FRONT PAGE
FACE-OFF

FRONT PAGE FACE-OFF

Jo Whittemore

ALADDIN M!X

NEW YORK   LONDON   TORONTO   SYDNEY

m!x aladdin

ALADDIN M!X

Simon & Schuster Children's Publishing Division

1230 Avenue of the Americas, New York, NY 10020

First Aladdin M!X edition March 2010

Text copyright © 2010 by Jo Whittemore

All rights reserved, including the right of reproduction in whole or in part in any form.

ALADDIN is a trademark of Simon & Schuster, Inc., and related logo is a registered trademark of Simon & Schuster, Inc.

ALADDIN M!X and related logo are registered trademarks of Simon & Schuster, Inc.

For information about special discounts for bulk purchases, please contact Simon & Schuster Special Sales at 1-866-506-1949 or business@simonandschuster.com.

The Simon & Schuster Speakers Bureau can bring authors to your live event. For more information or to book an event contact the Simon & Schuster Speakers Bureau at 1-866-248-3049 or visit our website at www.simonspeakers.com.

Designed by Lisa Vega

The text of this book was set in Garamond.

Manufactured in the United States of America

1111 OFF

10 9 8 7 6 5 4 3

Library of Congress Control Number 2009927097

ISBN 978-1-4169-9169-4

ISBN 978-1-4169-9890-3 (eBook)

For Cheryl,
the best critique partner the world has ever known

Acknowledgments

Always for God, family, and friends.

For my editor, Alyson Heller, who appreciates the hectic news world as much as I do.

For my agent, Jenn Laughran, who thinks I'm funny and helps me to see it.

For Michelle Andelman, who convinced me I had the talent to write this book.

For the Awesome Austin Writers, who I'm proud to call my friends.

For my Rochester posse and my Andover crew, who appreciate my second life.

And for ALD, JCH, and KPK, who always answer my phone calls, even when it's hazardous to their health.

Chapter One

In China a red envelope meant the owner had good luck and protection from evil. At Brighton Junior Academy a red envelope meant the owner had half a brain and way too many pairs of shoes.

I never expected to be in *that* group, but somehow, on the first day of seventh grade, one of those envelopes found its way to my locker.

Across the front of the envelope my name, Delilah James, flowed in fancy gold script, complete with a sparkling rhinestone dotting the *i*. As a writer for the school paper, I'd seen my name dozens of times in the byline, but never printed with quite as much pizzazz. Most girls would have squealed, taken their picture with the envelope, and framed it, but I just stared.

"Come on, Delilah!" Someone jabbed me in the ribs. "School ended five minutes ago, and I've *got* to have some real food." My best friend, Jenner, held up the candy necklace she'd been gnawing, now just a sticky elastic string holding some sugar loops. "I'm *this* close to cannibalism."

"Well, can you stop picturing me as a giant pork chop and look at *this*?" I stepped aside, revealing the envelope.

Jenner sucked in her breath, along with a partially chewed bit of candy. She coughed until I smacked her on the back. "No . . . way," she finally managed.

"I know."

She bent and studied my locker door, as if it had somehow produced the envelope on its own. "She would *never* send this."

"I know."

"She hates you!"

"I . . ." I frowned. "Well, I don't think she *hates* me. She just . . . mildly objects to my existence." I shrugged. "And maybe we're wrong. Maybe it's from someone else who has a thing for red envelopes."

"Ooooh!" Jenner's curly blond hair bounced as she leaned close and whispered, "It could be from a creepy

Valentine killer who's seven months behind. Or a creepy *Christmas* killer who's getting a head start on the season. *Or*—" I glared at her and she backed away. "Or something not involving any form of creepy holiday killer."

My best friend, queen of the macabre.

Jenner was overly fond of death, disease, and dismemberment. She'd once told me that if she couldn't make a career out of surfing (her first passion), then she wanted to be a grave digger.

The two of us turned to face the envelope.

It was time to get serious.

I plucked the envelope free, and a supercharged whiff of Chanel No. 5 hit me. In that instant I knew we weren't mistaken about the sender. Only one girl at Brighton Junior Academy wore that fragrance. Only one girl was *allowed* to wear that fragrance—Paige Sanders, president of the Debutantes.

And Jenner was right; Paige did hate me.

Of all the cliques that girls would push one another in front of a train to get into, the Debutantes had the longest line at the tracks. To be accepted meant instant popularity, but scoring the invite took an insane amount of brownnosing. The only exceptions to the admission process were the new president and her officers, who were chosen based on the number of girls they could crush beneath their wedge sandals.

I'd written an article on the whole affair, earning the wrath of the Debutantes, who didn't like the bad press *or* the fact that I called them "Little Debbies" (like the desserts, they were flaky, artificial, and hard to stomach). But I'd won an award for the piece *and* impressed the new student editor, who promoted me to lead reporter.

To be honest, that hadn't been half as surprising as the envelope in my hands.

"Open it." Jenner nudged me.

I ripped into the paper, and it exploded in a shower of star-shaped confetti and iridescent glitter. "Wow. This must be what happens when unicorns throw up."

"It's probably some decorative version of anthrax that'll make your lungs rupture and explode." Jenner brushed the excess off my hand. "Don't breathe too deep."

The card inside the envelope had "*You're Invited*!" written across the top in even more glitter, which clung to my fingertips and made the invitation sparkle. To add to all the shimmer and flair, the Little Debbies had jotted a personal note:

Dear Delilah,

It is our pleasure to formally announce your consideration for the Debutantes. Please join us tomorrow during study hall in the student lounge to discuss your potentially exciting future.

Paige's signature appeared at the bottom, followed by several names with various smiley faces and hearts dotting the *i*'s.

Jenner read over my shoulder and snorted.

I scanned the note several times and felt reality slipping further and further away. "I could *never* be one of them."

Jenner nodded in agreement. "You're smart *and* you have a good personality. Where would you fit in?"

I laughed and reached into the locker for my Thought Box, filing the invitation behind a cardboard divider labeled *Unexplained Phenomena*. "Congratulations, Paige. You've earned a coveted spot in my weirdo file."

"Shh. Listen." Jenner cupped her hand around her ear. "You can almost hear the cries of all the girls who couldn't score an invite."

In that moment of mock silence I actually *did* hear something: a commanding voice growing closer and clearer, punctuated by the *tap-tap-tap* of heels hitting the floor.

"And make sure the area's secure," said the voice, which I recognized as Paige's. She spoke in a nasal tone, as if she were pinching her nostrils to block out the smell of commoners. "I *don't* want any rejects trying to sneak in."

"Oh, that won't be an issue. We've got Aaron and Travis

on freak patrol." Another voice giggled, slightly out of breath.

"Good." There was no matching joy in Paige's voice. "And the pledge packets?"

A third voice chimed in, speaking at a rapid clip. "We've got pens, pins, forms, folders—"

"I didn't ask for a complete inventory," Paige cut in. "I just need to know if the packets are ready."

"Yes, totally" was the rapid response.

By this point, Paige and friends were passing the locker bay, and I realized the other voices I'd heard were Friend 1 and Friend 2, speed-walking to keep up with Paige's brisk pace.

Suddenly Paige paused mid-march and swiveled in my direction. Her blond hair swung around her shoulders like a shining silk curtain, and her eyes, one shade from violet, fixed on me.

"Delilah James." Her tone was neutral, devoid of the invite's glitter and confetti, and I wondered if one of her officers had sent it as a joke. But then Paige's lips parted into a smile broad enough for me to count every one of her perfect white teeth. "I'm so glad we ran into you!"

I looked to her friends, half expecting one of them to offer me a juicy, poisoned apple. Instead, they clutched at their clipboards and mirrored Paige's expression, toothy grins and all. "Um. Okay."

Paige waved just her fingertips at Jenner. "And good to see you, too . . ." She trailed off until one of her companions whispered in her ear. "Beatrice."

"I go by my last name, actually," said Jenner. "Beatrice is more for prune poppers."

Paige nodded while her companion whispered in her ear again. "Well, then, *Jenner*, it's good to see you, too, but you might want to rethink that fashion statement." She pointed to the lone piece of blue candy still hanging around Jenner's neck.

"Sorry. Let me get rid of it." Jenner brought the necklace to her mouth and crunched on it until the candy disappeared.

"And . . . now you're just wearing a piece of spit-soaked elastic." Paige's lip curled. "Even better."

Jenner winked at her. "I aim to please." To me, she waved and stepped back. "I'll see you in the courtyard."

"Strange girl . . . but cute," Paige commented, watching her go. "Too bad we didn't invite her to join the Debutantes."

"She's a surfer," commented one of Paige's friends. "And you're allergic to seaweed."

"Oh." Paige wrinkled her nose. "Never mind, then." She turned back to me. "So, you got our invitation."

I was still trying to make sense of their bizarre reason

for excluding Jenner. "Um . . . yeah. I did *not* see that coming."

Paige smiled and nodded at the confetti littering the ground. "Are you excited or what?" She held her arms open, as if expecting applause or a bouquet of roses.

"You made a mistake," I said.

Paige's arms snapped back to cross over her chest. "Interesting. I never make mistakes . . . but go on."

"Don't you remember that article I wrote last year? The one where I said less than stellar things about the *Little Debbies*?"

A flicker of annoyance crossed her face, but Paige smiled and relaxed. "Of course the *Débutantes* remember. That's exactly the reason we want you to join."

I glanced at her friends again, but they still stood with clipboards in hand, awaiting her next instruction. "I don't get it."

"Let me explain." Paige smiled sympathetically and plucked a stray hair off my blouse. "Jesus once said, 'If you can't beat 'em, join 'em—'"

I wrinkled my forehead. "Jesus didn't say that."

Paige rolled her eyes. "Confucius, then. Whatever." She gripped my shoulders. "The point is, Delilah, you have the power of the pen, and if you want to continue spreading *horrible* lies about us"—I opened my mouth to object, but she held up a palm—"we're powerless. So, since we can't beat you, we ask you to join us."

I frowned. "But that quote means *you* should join *me* . . . since you can't beat me."

Paige's expression darkened for a moment, but she forced a smile. "That's another reason you'd be an asset. You're so clever . . . and bold. You don't mind pointing out people's mistakes in front of others, even if it embarrasses them!"

Not even a machete could have hacked through the sarcasm hanging in the air. "Well, sorry, but I can't join," I said.

A clipboard hit the floor with a loud smack, and its pink-cheeked owner bent to pick it up. Paige scowled at the girl, then looked at me with an amused smile. "I . . . don't think I heard you correctly. Can you repeat that?"

I knew she'd heard the first time. This was just her way of offering me a second chance to keep from executing the biggest blunder in Brighton Junior Academy history.

"I decline your invitation to join the Debutantes," I said in my most formal tone.

Paige took a step back, as if I'd spat on her. "Seriously."

"Seriously," I said.

"But *nobody* declines!" exclaimed the girl who'd dropped her clipboard. She jabbed at it with her finger. "Out of thirty girls, you're the *only* one!"

"Cool." I peered at the clipboard. "Do I get a special trophy for that?"

Paige jerked the clipboard out of the other girl's hands and tucked it under one arm. "You don't want to turn this down, Delilah. You'd benefit as much as we would."

"How?" I asked. "By getting to call myself a Little Debbie?"

"Most people are grateful just to be called *Debutantes*," said Paige, stressing the last word so hard, I thought she might pull a muscle. "But we can help you achieve your heart's desire." She reached into her backpack and held up a teen magazine.

I read the headlines. "Well, I *would* like clearer skin in five days . . . but that's not my heart's desire."

The magazine crinkled under Paige's fingers, and she pressed her lips together before speaking in a quiet, girl-on-the-edge tone. "I'm talking about being a journalist, Delilah. That's your big dream, isn't it? To write long, boring articles about world affairs and the grayhouse effect someday?"

"Greenhouse," I corrected. "Your point?"

"You have to start somewhere," said Paige. "And we have access to information that would make *US Weekly* jealous."

I tried to appear uninterested, but Paige had a point. If anyone knew what was happening at Brighton, it was the

Little Debbies . . . and they didn't share their secrets with just anyone.

I cleared my throat. "Out of curiosity . . . what sort of information are we talking about?"

Paige shrugged, but the corners of her mouth curved upward. "I guess you won't know unless you become a Debutante." She leaned closer to me. "But I can tell you this. One of our classmates is about to be spending a little time in juvie for her sticky fingers."

"Shoplifting," translated Friend 1. She immediately quieted after a look from Paige.

"And not even *good* shoplifting," continued Paige. "In a roomful of Coach, the girl went for Nine West!"

I bit my lip and fought for calm. "Oh. Is that all?"

A lead-in like *that* almost wrote its own story, and I had no doubt Paige already knew who the girl was. If my first article as lead reporter could be about preteen shoplifting and its consequences from an actual offender . . .

Daydreaming wasn't my thing, but I allowed myself a hypothetical. In it I was holding the Junior Global Journalist Award, thanking my mom for her support and my late father for his inspiration.

My dad had died when I was still in grade school. He'd been one of the best journalists in the country, always praised for his original stories and attention to detail in his research.

He was my idol; I wouldn't exactly be following in his footsteps if the Little Debbies fed me all my information.

I sighed and shook my head. "It's tempting, but I'd rather do this on my own."

Paige stared at me for a moment before nodding. "I understand." She gestured to Friend 1 and Friend 2. "We'll see you in the lounge during study hall tomorrow."

"Wait." I waved my hands. "Didn't you hear me? I'm not interested." I thrust the invite at her, and she regarded it with an amused smile.

"Keep it. I've seen your future." She arched one eyebrow and turned to walk away. "By tomorrow afternoon you'll be holding on to that invitation for dear life."

Chapter Two

Paige has seen your future?
She can't even see her *own*
future as a Macy's per-
fume spritzer." Jenner let
out her trademark laugh that was
part hyena, part mule, and altogether
terrifying to children and woodland
creatures.

We were walking home from
school, and I'd just filled her in on
my discussion with Paige, including
the mysterious shoplifter, but Jenner
was focused on one thing.

"Wait!" She grabbed my arm and
gazed at me with wide, dramatic
eyes. "I'll bet the Little Debbies have
a time machine!"

I *did* crack a smile at that. "Man, the rich kids get all the best stuff."

Jenner unwrapped a lollipop ring and slid it on her finger. "You should have Major build one for *you*," she said as she popped the ring into her mouth.

Major was Major Paulsen, my soon-to-be-stepfather, a tall man with perfect posture and a salt-and-pepper buzz cut. When he wasn't caught up in nauseating romance with my mom, he worked on government defense technology.

"With the projects his team handles, they probably *could* build me a time machine," I said. "Then at least I'd know what was coming."

The candy ring popped out of Jenner's mouth. "Don't tell me you actually believe Paige."

I pointed to a group of squealing girls ahead of us, one of whom was clutching a familiar red envelope. "They *all* want to be Little Debbies, and if they think it'll help their chances, they'll give up any secret they know."

"But about *you*?" Jenner cast me a dubious look. "No offense, but you're not that interesting."

I shoved her playfully. "It doesn't have to be *about* me, dummy. It just has to *affect* me."

Jenner sucked on her ring and looked thoughtful. "Something with the newspaper?"

I nodded. "Paige knows it's the only thing at school I care about."

"Well, she's crazy if she thinks *that'll* go wrong." Jenner smiled around her emerald-colored candy. "Not while the editor's smooching your sneakers, anyway."

I gave a modest shrug, but I knew she was right.

Ben Hines, the student editor, had been crushing on me since I'd saved him from the Swirlie Bandit in sixth grade. He was the shortest kid in our class and let his mom wipe his face with saliva-soaked Kleenex. Naturally that made him a prime target for attack.

At the time, I'd been trying to unmask the Swirlie Bandit, but nobody in the boy's bathroom would say anything to me except "Get out!" When I finally managed to sneak in, the Swirlie Bandit showed up to dunk Ben, and I exposed him in person *and* in the paper. The boy had been smart enough to hide his face . . . but not his jersey with the name "Marcus" on it. Nowadays he was probably serving time in juvie with kids named Knuckles and the Impaler.

"I should try and find Marcus for a follow-up article," I said.

Jenner snorted. "Somehow I doubt he'd talk to you." She tugged my hair. "Weren't his last words 'I hate you, crazy redhead'?"

"Yes, but the Little Debbies hate me too," I reminded her, "and look how *that* turned out."

Jenner shuddered. "Geez, what a freaky cult. I'm *so* glad you didn't join."

"Having their info would have rocked," I admitted, "but I can come up with stories on my own."

"Exactly." Jenner nodded. "Because *you* are a future Junior Global Journalist."

"Speaking of which"—I rubbed my hands together—"it's time for the debut edition of the paper! Which article is more award-worthy? X-ray machines for frogs or desperate dating behavior?"

"X-rays, definitely." Jenner held up a hand. "*Unless* the desperate dating involves sending someone a severed thumb."

"No, but almost as gross." I stepped closer to whisper. "Two weeks ago at the mall, I saw Renee Mercer wearing dark sunglasses and a wig."

Jenner's eyebrows furrowed. "Okay . . ."

"She was hiding behind this big pillar in the food court, watching her ex-boyfriend eat an ice-cream cone. He couldn't finish it, so he threw it away. As soon as he left, Renee ran over to the waste bin and pulled out the ice-cream cone."

Jenner's jaw dropped. "She didn't—"

I nodded. "She ate it."

Jenner flinched. "That's an *entirely* different kind of creepy."

I pulled a spiral notepad from my back pocket and read aloud. "Gobbling his garbage? It's time to move on."

"Uh . . . no." Jenner took my notepad and ripped off the top page. "You're *not* writing an article about people who can't let go. Especially Renee. She'll pound you into oblivion!"

"She wouldn't be the focus of the article," I explained. "Just an example."

Jenner raised an eyebrow.

"An anonymous example."

Jenner refused to blink, and I groaned. "Come on! People care more about dating than frogs."

"Yeah, that's a good quote for your tombstone," she said. "We should order now so it'll be ready when Renee's done ripping your head off."

"Fine. Why don't we stop by Ben's house and ask him which *he* thinks is better?"

Jenner smirked at me. "You just want a chance to hear him say you're the lead reporter again."

"Well, I didn't see him all summer," I said. "He went to France for the first half and then Major made us go to Yosemite for most of the second."

"Fine." Jenner sighed. "I have time to kill."

"Great! Let me just drop off my stuff and tell Major." Mom was out of the country on business for two weeks, and she'd invited Major over to "bond" with me. . . . A nice way of saying she'd found a free babysitter.

We reached my house, and Jenner followed me into the hallway. "Major?" I called.

"In the kitchen!" bellowed a gravelly voice. "Come tell me what you want for dinner."

Jenner poked me. "He cooks? When it's just me and *my* dad, he never cooks."

I rolled my eyes. "Don't be impressed. Everything he makes comes from a box with 'Just add water!' on the outside."

"Yeah, but . . ." Jenner sniffed the air. "At least he makes cake."

When I walked into the kitchen, Major had an assortment of boxes and bags lined up on the counter. It was a little weird to see him wearing an apron over his military fatigues, but Major liked to stay professional at all times. Even his pajamas were government issue.

"Girls, hello!" he boomed. "How was school?"

"Are you baking cake?" Jenner asked.

Major grinned and pointed to a fluffy white monster with brown crust. "Angel food cake. Would you like a slice?"

Jenner's eyes lit up. "Yes, *please.*"

Major grabbed a plate for her. "How about you, Delilah?"

"Just a small one," I said. "We're heading back out in a minute."

Major put down the plate and pulled a slip of paper from his pocket, studying it for a moment before glancing up at me. "Do you have any homework?"

"Not on the first day of school." I unzipped my backpack so he could see inside, and Major wrinkled his nose.

"*What* is that smell?"

I took a whiff of Paige's signature scent, which was starting to overwhelm the aroma of baked cake. "Oh, just perfume." I held out my hands for a plate of spongy goodness, but Major kept it just out of reach.

"You know how your mother feels about perfume, Delilah." He referred to his paper again. "Not until . . . you're in high school."

"It's not mine!" I whipped the Little Debbie invite out of my bag. "It's from this."

Major took the invite from me, his lips moving as he read until they eventually curved into a smile. "Well, this is great, Delilah!"

"Yeah, but I'm not going to join," I said.

Major clucked his tongue and passed me a slice of cake. "That's too bad. The social skills you develop now will shape your future." He sounded as if he'd memorized the words out of a parenting manual.

"My future is journalism, Major." I ripped off a chunk of cake and popped it into my mouth. "And being part of a snob society won't help."

Major leaned against the counter. "I hate to break this to you, Delilah, but the 'snob society' is *very* influential in the news world. Who do you think owns all the magazines?"

"It *is* all about who you know," agreed Jenner. "The student editor has a crush on Delilah and now she's the lead—" She shrank back under my glare of indignation. "Sorry, but he has cake!"

"A crush?" Major frowned and left the room, returning a moment later with a blue binder. "Who is this guy, Delilah?"

"His name's Ben Hines, and Jenner and I are going to his house *right now* to talk about the paper." I crammed the rest of the cake into my mouth and shot Jenner a pointed look.

"Just a moment." Major held up one hand while he flipped through the binder. "Hines, you said?"

"Yeah. Why?" I craned my neck and saw a page full of guy's faces and names, all bordered by green, yellow, or red marker.

I let out a horrified gasp. "Major! You cut up my yearbook?"

"At ease, Delilah. They're just *photocopied* from your year-book," he said. "I don't know your classmates as well as your mother, so I had her fill me in, and I made a few judgment calls of my own." He tapped Ben's picture. "Luckily, he's in the green. I approve."

I just stared at the pages in disbelief. Only Major would categorize my peers by threat level. I was surprised *every* guy wasn't outlined in red.

"What happens if they're yellow?" Jenner pointed to a picture of a kid I'd seen maybe a dozen times at school.

"Delilah's allowed to spend a maximum of two hours in their company, provided there's an adult chaperone."

I made a face. "You're so weird, Major. We're gonna go meet Ben now."

"What about dinner?" he asked.

"Pizza!" I pulled Jenner out the door, cake still in her hand.

"Remember," Major called after us, "he may be green, but he's still a teen!"

"You know, Ben doesn't really look like his picture any-more," Jenner said as we walked up the Hines' driveway.

I paused on the bottom step to their porch. "What do you mean?"

"Well, he's taller now, and I saw him at the beach when

he got back from France. He's pretty tan."

I tried to picture Ben soaking up rays on the beach, but all I could imagine was his mom hovering over him with an umbrella and yelling at him to put on sunscreen. "I still don't think Major needs to worry."

I knocked on the front door and waited a few moments before pushing it open.

"Ben?"

Something thumped on the second floor, followed by a rolling thunder of footsteps across the landing and down the stairs.

"Delilah?" His eyes peeped around the edge of the staircase, and then his entire head appeared. "Hey! What's up?"

He bounded toward me, grinning, but I couldn't respond. My jaw had reached the floor, and my tongue threatened to flop out.

Either my standards had lowered, or Ben had gotten cuter over the summer.

The tips of his hair were frosted, and his skin was a gorgeous bronze. His clothes—jeans and a polo shirt—were casual and, for once, didn't look as if his mom had picked them out.

"Ben! You . . . you look awesome!" I sputtered.

He laughed, and I noticed his voice had dropped an octave. "So do you. How was your summer?" He hugged me, smelling of hot guy and potential boyfriend.

"How was *your* summer?" I stepped back and gestured to him. "You look so different!"

He chuckled again and blushed, the pink barely visible against his skin. "I had some help. My hair was starting to get out of control, so I had to tame it . . . and I spent a lot of time outdoors."

"Wow. All I spent my time doing was . . ." Suddenly I realized how boring my summer had been. "Um . . . wrestling alligators."

Jenner pinched me, but to Ben's credit, he merely smiled. "Hey, wait right here. I've got a surprise for you!"

"Okay." I smiled and put an arm around Jenner's shoulders. The second Ben disappeared, my fingers pulled at the latest candy necklace around her throat, letting it snap back in place.

"Ow! What was that for?"

"You told me Ben grew!" I hissed. "You didn't say he grew *hotter*!"

Jenner rubbed her neck. "Why do *you* care? You're waist-deep in imaginary alligators!"

"I . . . well, I don't *care*." Someone must have turned up the thermostat. The room suddenly felt ten degrees warmer.

"Aww. Kodak moment." Jenner held up an invisible camera and clicked the shutter, taking shots from various angles.

"Delilah's first crush on something other than journalism."

I sighed. "He is a smottie, isn't he?"

"Smottie" was a Jenner term for a guy who was smart *and* a hottie.

Jenner tilted her hand from side to side. "Semi-smottie. You can do better."

Ben poked his head around the stairwell again, smiling. "Are you ready for my surprise? It's a good one."

"Yes! Yes!" Jenner and I clapped and whistled, and Ben cleared his throat ceremoniously.

"May I present to you . . . Ms. Ava Piquet!" He gestured to the top of the staircase, and a pair of long, slender legs in Roman sandals emerged.

I stopped clapping, and Jenner let her cheering trail off with a dying "Whooo . . . hoo."

The leggy sandals at the top of the stairs stepped down to reveal a strapless red sundress, boasting a model-thin figure.

"Please, let her have a horse face," I whispered under my breath. "Or a unibrow."

But as the rest of Ava Piquet strolled into view, I saw a beautiful girl with raven-colored hair and ivory skin. Her lips, which refused to smile, were the exact color of her dress.

"Ava, these are my friends Delilah and Jenner," said Ben.

She acknowledged both of us with the slightest nod and coiled one of her arms through Ben's. "How do you do," she said in a thick French accent.

"Nice to meet you." Jenner looked at Ben. "So, is this your . . . cousin?"

"Please." Ava's perfectly sculpted shoulders quivered with amusement. "I am Benjamin's girlfriend."

Ben grinned at us some more. "I met her when I was in France, and I convinced her to try a foreign exchange program."

"Neat," I said in a tight voice. "So, when is she going back?" Jenner elbowed me. "I mean, how long is she here?"

"For the entire school year!" Ben drew Ava close. "But that's not the best part of it!" He gazed admiringly at her. "Delilah . . ." He paused for effect. "Ava's going to share the lead reporter position with you!"

For a moment, silence enveloped the room as everyone watched me expectantly.

"Wow." I swallowed hard. "I'm so excited . . . I could just . . . throw up."

And I did.

Chapter Three

China rattled in the cabinets, and pictures nearly flew off the walls as I stormed back into my house.

"Argggh! Un-freaking-believable!"

Major glanced up from where he was reading the paper, not looking nearly concerned enough. "What happened?"

I pointed out the front door with a shaking finger. "The French . . . are invading!"

"What?" Major regarded me with wonderment. "What's all over the front of your sweater?"

"Puke!" I jerked my sweater off

and threw it on the floor. "I threw up on a French girl."

"Why?" Again, Major seemed bewildered but not particularly alarmed about my random regurgitation.

"She . . . just . . . ruined my life," I said through clenched teeth.

"Ah. Well . . ." Major reached for the slip of paper in his pocket again, and I snatched it from him.

"Would you stop looking at the cheat sheet and start caring a little more?!"

That outburst *was* enough to get a stronger reaction out of Major . . . but not the one I wanted. He folded his newspaper with a hard crease and slapped it on the coffee table, then turned to shrivel me with a stern gaze. "I beg your pardon."

"Sorry," I said quickly, putting the cheat sheet back into one of his hands. "But this is a big deal to me, especially with the huge embarrassment factor involved."

Major stared at me for a moment, then steered me toward my bedroom, pointing at the bed. "Sit."

He settled himself into my desk chair and studied me solemnly for a moment before speaking. "Your mother left me several parenting manuals, but none of them explain how to deal with a vomit-covered girl shouting about a French invasion."

I blushed and stared at my lap.

"Why don't we start from the moment you left for Ben's?" said Major. "I have a feeling he's somehow involved in this too."

Pulling my legs as close to my chest as possible, I told Major what had happened, leaving out the details of Ben's sudden hotness lest his picture earn a red outline in Major's book.

"So, out of the blue, she becomes his favorite reporter and just swoops in to take the spot that *I* worked so hard for." I pounded my fist into the mattress. "It's not fair."

Major scratched his chin. "Well, I'm sure he wouldn't have selected this girl if she weren't qualified. Has she received any accolades?"

"I don't know!" I couldn't help my irritation that he hadn't taken my side . . . again. Clearly, I'd have to make a few corrections to the parenting manual.

"Is she as interested in journalism as you are?" he asked.

"I have no idea."

"Is it possible she was lead reporter for her own school paper?"

"I . . . don't . . . know!" I flopped back on my bed and covered my face with a pillow.

Major got to his feet and paced the carpet in front of me. "Do you know one of the first things they teach you in military intelligence?"

"A hundred ways to kill a man with your pinky." My voice was muffled through the down pillow.

"Know . . . your . . . adversary." He tapped my leg to emphasize each word. "If you think this girl is a threat, you need to learn everything you can about her. Neutralize the threat. I'm sure you've done it before."

I propped myself on my elbows. He was right. When I'd written the article about the Little Debbies, I'd studied them for months. And now *they* were coming to *me* with offers to join them. I squeezed past him to my computer and pulled up a search engine, punching in Ava's name.

Major patted me on the back. "I'll leave you to work and bring your dinner in later." I barely heard him leave.

The moment Ava's name hit the Web, a flurry of results came back, most in French, some in English—to my chagrin, all referring to a twelve-year-old journalist.

The very first listing was Ava's own website, with her unsmiling mug surrounded by links written in French that turned to English with the skim of a mouse. Her bio read like an eighty-year-old's, describing her love of crosswords and knitting, but she must have updated it regularly, because it mentioned her involvement in the foreign exchange program. Overall I wasn't impressed with Mademoiselle Piquet . . . until I clicked the link labeled "Awards."

In the center of *that* page was another picture of Ava,

smiling this time, with a gold medal the size of a hubcap around her neck. Beneath the picture a caption read "Induction into Junior Global Journalists."

I jerked away from the computer, as if it had given me an electric shock. My dad had been inducted into the Junior Global Journalists when he was fourteen, and I hoped to be chosen when I was thirteen. Judging by the date on the photo, however, Ava had been inducted this year—at *twelve*.

While it relieved me to know Ben *had* chosen her for a good reason, I now realized just how massive a threat Ava posed to the rest of my year. She would need to be neutralized, as Major had said, but just knowing *this* enemy wouldn't be enough.

The next morning at school, I tried to come up with story ideas that would amaze and astound. My biggest advantage was knowing everything about Brighton and its students. They didn't care about crosswords and knitting; they cared about stuff that affected their daily lives. School, dating, *normal* hobbies . . . all these things could help me elbow out the competition if I chose the right topic.

While my teachers droned on with lesson plans, I scribbled on my spiral notepad, snatching fresh ideas from nearby conversations.

By the time journalism rolled around, I was armed with

enough material to get me through the meeting and hopefully put Ava to shame.

But when I reached the journalism room, my confidence wavered. Ava and Ben were already there, standing in the doorway. Or rather, *he* stood and she clung to him like some parasitic fashionista. She was wearing a shapeless purple dress that hung limply off her shoulders and a hefty silver bracelet that could knock someone unconscious if used as a weapon.

Yet I could only focus on one thing when I saw them— the new, hot Ben.

The new, hot Ben who had seen me throw up.

He'd acted as if it were okay, but I had a feeling he and Ava had probably discussed embarrassing nicknames to call me afterward.

I took a steadying breath and held my head high as I prepared to walk past them. My best bet was to act like throwing up in public was the norm and *they* were the strange ones for not doing it too. "Good morning." I smiled indulgently at them and then stared ahead, not daring to look back until I heard my name.

"Hey, Delilah." Ben disentangled himself from Ava and followed me inside. "Are you feeling okay today?" He placed a hand on my back, and the skin there went numb from his touch. I needed to say something before my tongue did the same.

"I'm fine," I said. "In fact, I'm *really, really* sorry . . ."

Ben moved his hand around to squeeze my arm. "Don't be. I shouldn't have sprung the whole thing on you like that. Not after you'd just eaten, anyway." He grinned, and I ducked my head but returned his smile.

"Listen, I better join Mrs. Bradford before class starts." Ben nodded to our faculty advisor and left to sit with her at the front of the room.

When I turned to watch Ava's reaction, my eyebrows jumped an inch up my forehead.

During newspaper meetings the editor sat at the end of the table, while the faculty advisor sat to the left and the lead reporter sat to the right. By chance or by choice, Ava had chosen the chair to Ben's right.

The seat being warmed by her bony posterior was supposed to be *mine.*

She watched me with a defiant look in her eyes, but I merely settled into the chair beside Mrs. Bradford's. "Hello, Ava," I said. "Thrilled to see you again."

Ava smirked and tossed a plastic shopping bag at me. "I brought this for you. I don't want you to get 'thrilled' all over the desk."

She seemed so amused at my discomfort, so pleased to be interfering in my life, that I couldn't help myself.

I smiled and shook the plastic bag open. "I thought this

was your purse. Isn't that the theme of your outfit? Recycling?"

"I don't know *what* you mean." She gave her hair a dramatic, slow-motion toss, and I pointed to her dress.

"The tablecloth you're wearing. Did everyone finish eating before you grabbed it?"

Ava's upper lip curled with malice. "It is a *sack* dress. And if you knew anything about fashion, you would know they are the hottest thing this season."

I nodded. "I've heard it's what *all* the tables are wearing."

"Hey, Delilah!" Jenner dropped into the seat on my other side and gave me a squeeze. "Are you feeling better? I tried to call your house, but Major said you weren't available."

"Oh, yeah. I'm fine. I was busy working on ideas for the paper." I fanned the stack of notepad pages at Jenner, making sure Ava could see them too.

"You might have a hundred ideas," said Ava with a wave of her hand, "but if none of them are good, you might as well have nothing."

"Oh, Delilah's ideas are always great." Jenner fished in her pocket and pulled out a candy necklace. "She's won a bunch of awards, and she'll be a Junior Global Journalist soon." She smiled at me encouragingly, but I blushed and concentrated on my notes.

"She'll be one *soon*?" Ava purred. "Interesting. You know—"

"It really doesn't matter what awards we've won," I blurted. "What matters is what the readers think. It's all about giving them the news they want and need to hear."

"*Very* inspirational." Ava rolled her eyes. "I can see why they let you play reporter."

I wondered how much of her ego-swollen head would fit into the plastic bag. "I don't *play* reporter. It's not a *game*."

"Then you wouldn't mind a little friendly competition." Ava raised an eyebrow. "Would you?"

Chapter Four

At that moment, I would have preferred to sit as far from Ava as the edge of the continent would allow, but I wasn't ready to just give up the lead reporter spot. Especially not with my editor/potential boyfriend trapped in her claws.

The room buzzed with conversation as students compared summer vacations and plans for the new school year, until Ben motioned for quiet.

"To anyone who was here last year, welcome back. And to anyone who just joined the *Brighton Bugle* . . ." He paused and grinned. "What took you so long?"

Several people laughed.

Ben turned to a dry erase board and began writing newspaper sections, with names of the staffers who handled them. "Since a lot of our writers graduated last year, we have some people moving up. Headline news will be handled by Delilah James and Ava Piquet."

"Delilah and who?" yelled someone in the back.

With a fierce hair toss Ava rose and faced the rest of the table. "Ava Piquet, Junior Global Journalist."

Jenner snorted, but when Ava whirled to look at her, she smiled up innocently, candy necklace stuffed in her mouth.

"Ava is an exchange student from France, and she reported for her own paper back home," said Ben.

"Does she even know how to *write* in English?" someone else asked.

"Of course I do!" Ava shot back. "I have studied your language since I was little, and I am also fluent in Latin."

"That'll be handy—two thousand years ago," I said.

Ava's eyes frosted over as they fixed on mine. "They say Latin is a mystery to stupid people. I guess they are right."

Mrs. Bradford cleared her throat. "Let's focus, ladies. We only have forty-five minutes."

Ben continued introducing the other new staffers and returned to the board when he was done. "We'll start with the headline news." He looked at me and smiled. "Delilah, what's your debut piece?"

I was about to answer but thought better of it. If I let Ava go first, she would no doubt suggest some lame article, like "Ten Reasons I Wish I'd Stayed in France." Nobody would care, and it would show Mrs. Bradford *and* Ben that she didn't have her finger on the pulse of the school. Then I could follow up her idea with something that would be of interest to everyone . . . like X-ray machines for frogs.

I pointed to Ava. "Why don't we let the new student go first? I'd love to hear from the mind of a Junior Global Journalist."

Ava was clever enough to regard me with some suspicion, but she leaned forward and addressed the crowd. "I wanted to write my first article on an issue that is affecting more and more young people." She lifted her chin and sniffed imperiously. "In this country, anyway."

I tilted back in my chair and stifled a yawn. "We already covered the obesity topic last year. We even did a focus on stealth junk foods because *some* people thought Sno Balls were healthy." I stared pointedly at Jenner, who stuck out her tongue.

"On top of being delicious, they're covered with coconut," she said. "And what's the first thing people search for when they're stranded on a desert island?"

Ava smacked her palm on the table and Jenner jumped. "I am not talking about obesity. I am talking about something *much* bigger that has happened to someone at *this* school." She paused for emphasis, and the room fell silent. "Juvenile detention . . . for shoplifting!"

The front legs of my chair slammed into the floor. "What!"

Ava's mouth curved into a smile, but she didn't answer. With the commotion that followed, nobody would have heard her, anyway.

"It's Gina Mueller! I know it! Nobody who brings a sack lunch could afford shoes like that."

"It's Abbey Houston. I saw her shopping for an orange prison jumpsuit."

"They don't wear those in juvie."

"Ohhh. Then she has really bad taste."

Even Jenner had her own ideas ("An evil twin!"), but I sat quietly, staring at Ava. If nobody else had recognized the mystery student yet, I found it hard to believe that Ava, an outsider, had. And somehow I doubted any preteen purse thief would confide in a stranger with such a *charming* personality.

The only person who could have possibly shared this information with Ava was the same person who had shared it with me.

While Ava basked in the glory of all her attention, I casually knocked my pen off the table and bent to retrieve it. After a glance around to make sure nobody was watching, I ducked under the table and leaned toward Ava's book bag. A familiar perfume filled the air, and the corner of a red envelope peeked out of the side pocket.

"Paige . . . that double-crosser!" I whispered.

"Delilah?" Mrs. Bradford's head appeared under the table. "Are you okay?"

"Oh! Yes!" I tried to straighten up, still under the table, and whacked the back of my skull. "I was just . . . getting my pen." My eyes watered as I shifted backward, rubbing my scalp. "So, who's the shoplifter?"

"Ava doesn't want to name names." Ben gazed admiringly at his girlfriend, Saint Pompous. "She'll be quoting the student anonymously out of respect."

"Or because she doesn't know who it is yet," I said under my breath.

"Okay, Delilah. You're up!" Ben held his marker at the ready. "What's the scoop?"

All eyes were on me, but my eyes were on Ava's headline on the board: "Middle School Misfits." As much as I hated to admit it, her piece was going to get a lot of attention . . . way more than frog dissection.

"Mine . . . also has to deal with student issues," I said.

Jenner knew where I was headed and cleared her throat loudly, giving a cough that sounded like "Don't!"

I ignored her and continued to look at Ben. "I decided to do a piece on desperate dating behavior."

Jenner coughed even louder and slapped the table.

"Beatrice, this is why I don't like you chewing those candy necklaces!" said Mrs. Bradford. "Does anyone know the Heimlich?"

"I'm fine!" Jenner protested. "Delilah, go ahead with your funeral . . . uh . . . idea."

I knew I was about to make her head explode, but I had no other choice. "Well, this summer I saw Renee Mercer eating out of a trash can—"

"Bwa-ha-ha!"

The first raucous laugh came from somewhere in the back of the room. Several other people joined in.

It wasn't the initial response I'd hoped for, but at least I'd gotten some attention.

"That's not the whole story," I said. "See, it was an ice-cream cone that belonged to her ex-boyfriend, and she was stalking him at the mall."

Now everyone was chattering, even more so than about the shoplifting teen. I'd attached a face and name to the situation, something Ava *hadn't* done, making my story seem raw and real. With the buzz I was already building, the article was sure to explode once it reached the student body, lifting me to Junior Global Journalist acclaim.

And then I heard a voice at the end of the table say five dooming words: "Wait until Renee hears this."

A girl from the sports section, who I now recognized as one of Renee's lacrosse teammates, whipped her cell phone out of her purse.

Beside me, I heard the smack of palm against forehead as Jenner sang, "I toooold you."

Other kids caught on to Lacrosse Girl's idea, and soon thumbs started to fly across keypads, as the story of Renee's summer adventure was texted to other classrooms . . . and of course, to Renee herself.

"Wait! Whoa!" I leaned across the table, though Lacrosse Girl was still several arm lengths from me. "This conversation doesn't need to leave the room yet. It's just an idea!"

"A bad idea!" chimed in Jenner.

I glared at her and she shrugged. "I'm only trying to help."

"I wasn't going to use Renee's name in the article," I insisted. "My sources were going to be anonymous . . . like Ava's!" I pointed at her, hoping to spread a little of my impending doom.

Jenner had been right. It was one thing to take on the Little Debbies, girls I could beat down with a wet noodle;

Renee Mercer was an entirely different beast. She was going to make me the school's first obituary listing.

"Cell phones away before I take them away!" shouted Mrs. Bradford. "We've obviously got some great articles for our next issue, but Delilah"—she turned to me—"you *will* need to keep your sources anonymous when you write your piece."

I flopped back into my seat and groaned. "If I live to write it."

As the meeting continued, I became aware of a strange chain reaction at the opposite end of the table. It started with the girl who'd texted Renee.

I watched her check her phone, then clap a hand to her mouth and giggle. The boy to her right leaned close, and she showed him the message. His eyes widened, and the boy to *his* right leaned over so the first boy could whisper to him. The second boy passed the message to the girl beside him, and *she* tapped Jenner on the shoulder.

I tried to read the girl's lips, though I knew the message couldn't hold anything promising. A moment later, my suspicions were confirmed. Jenner cringed, scribbled on a piece of paper, and passed it to me.

Renee is going to tie you to the tetherball pole and bat you around.

I raised an eyebrow and Jenner scribbled on the paper some more.

She's going to the gym right now *to tape up her hands.*

I frowned in confusion, and Jenner mimed a few boxing punches.

Just then, my sense of self-preservation kicked in.

I grabbed my book bag and stood up. "Mrs. Bradford, I want to talk to the headmaster about my idea. May I go now?"

Mrs. Bradford checked her watch. "I think that should be okay. Did you have any more input for the meeting?"

"Oh . . . I'm sure I've said enough." I glanced at Jenner, who crossed her fingers and smiled hopefully.

My attention drifted from her to Ava, who was also smiling . . . but with a glimmer of satisfaction in her eyes.

"See you later, Delilah." Ben walked me to the door. "And sorry again about the lead reporter thing," he whispered.

Despite my situation, I was still *very* aware of this new Ben. He had leaned in close to talk, and I could smell his cologne. His arms seemed more muscular than they had that morning, as if he'd been lifting weights instead of dry erase markers.

"It's okay," I whispered back, trying to inhale his scent at the same time. "I'm just glad *you're* in charge."

Ben turned a pleased pink as he stepped away. "Try and stay out of Renee's sight, okay? I don't think she'll be too happy with you."

I rolled my eyes. "Please. Renee Mercer's nothing. I stood

up to the Swirlie Bandit. You don't think I can stand up to *her?*"

Ben grinned. "Just be careful."

I laughed and waved him off, but the second he closed the door, I sprinted down the hall in the direction of the headmaster's office. I wasn't sure of the school's official policy, but I was pretty sure students couldn't assault one another there. Plus, it was the opposite direction from the gym, where Renee was probably loading her pockets with shotputs to hurl at me.

I paused to catch my breath and survey my surroundings. With the exception of a wandering sixth grader, the hallway was empty.

Someone tapped me hard on the shoulder, and I screamed.

"Looking for me?" asked a male voice.

I stopped screaming and turned to find a dark-haired guy frowning down at me. His eyes sparked like bits of black flint, and he crossed his arms over a chest broad enough to double as a movie screen.

My mouth opened just enough to allow one word to escape. "Marcus!"

Chapter Five

I bet you never thought you'd see me again." Marcus, the Swirlie Bandit, smirked and fixed me with a hard stare.

I smiled at him weakly. "Actually, with the kind of day I'm having, I should have expected it."

Marcus took a step toward me and stretched his shoulders back, tilting his head to both sides so that his neck cracked ominously. "Well, you and I need to have a little talk."

"Oh! Heh. That would be great." I glanced around him, looking for the wandering sixth grader or someone else who could bear witness to my demise.

A few seconds later, someone even larger than Marcus came thundering down the hall. Renee Mercer was approaching fast . . . too fast for me to make an escape. The air seemed to vibrate with her every movement, sending shock waves of hate in my direction.

"Ack!" I grabbed Marcus by the shoulders and spun him around, placing him between me and the steadily advancing, steadily *growing* Renee. "Uhhhh . . . listen, I'd love to fight it out with you, but there's someone after me right now with a *much* fresher grudge . . . and she bench-presses small children."

Marcus looked at one of his shoulders, and I realized I was still clutching them.

"Sorry." I smoothed down his wrinkled sleeves. "Can we schedule this confrontation for a later date?" I pulled my spiral notepad out of my pocket. "When's good for you?"

"Huh?" Marcus raised his head and stared at me, baffled. "Um . . . tomorrow before school, I guess."

"That's great! Perfect!" I jotted a reminder for both of us and handed one over. "Now, you might want to step out of the way. She's built up a pretty good momentum and can probably take you down with me."

Marcus shifted to one side and glanced behind him. Renee loomed larger than ever. "Whoa!"

"Yeah, keep shouting that," I said. "She's about the size

of a Clydesdale. Maybe she follows commands like one." I leaned against the wall and stretched my calves. Then I pulled my knees to my chest. "Is it true they don't give you forks in juvie?"

"I've never been to juvie," said Marcus. "What are you doing?"

"Stretching." I knew Renee would come at me with fists flying, but I wasn't going down without a fight. "I took two weeks of self-defense during PE last year. They have to be worth something." I practiced a few punches. "If you weren't in juvie, where were you?"

"A different private school." Marcus grabbed my fists and moved my thumbs to the outside of my fingers. "You won't break them this way."

"Thanks. Although you realize you're giving me tips to beat *you*, too."

Marcus smirked. "I'm sure I'll fight you off somehow."

Renee was now within threat-issuing distance, and she unleashed a volley of them. "I'm going to kill you, Delilah! You won't live to see high school! You won't live to see the end of the day!"

"You should go," I told Marcus. "I don't want my blood to get all over your nice shirt."

"Actually, I want to see how this turns out." He settled himself against the wall.

Renee roared and charged toward me, reeling back one arm. Suddenly Paige Sanders emerged from a nearby locker bay and stepped in front of me, blocking my body with her own.

Renee ground to a halt inches from Paige's diva stance, as if smacking into an invisible wall. "What . . . what are you doing here, Sanders?"

"Sanctuary," said Paige. "While Delilah is pledging the Debutantes, she's under our protection." She glanced at Marcus. "From *all* enemies."

Marcus smirked at me. "You're going to be a Debutante?"

"Of course she is." Paige fixed her eyes on mine. "If she knows what's good for her."

Trapped in a triangle of evil, I couldn't so much as come up with a sarcastic response. "Ummm . . ."

I needed to best Ava if I wanted to get my position back *and* save Ben from her clutches. As it stood, she had the power of the Little Debbies behind her, and all the secrets they possessed. If I agreed to join them, only for a little while, I could even the playing field and avoid meeting the business end of Renee Mercer's fist *plus* whatever Marcus had planned for me.

Three pairs of eyes were still watching me.

"Well?" Renee leaned over Paige's shoulder, her brim stone breath heating my face.

"Well, if anyone needs me"—I cleared my throat—"I guess I'll be in the student lounge this afternoon. With the Little Debbies."

I'd never considered a building capable of evil, but as the student lounge loomed before me, I almost heard its hinged shutters cackle with glee. Signs outside the building urged me to use my "inside voice," which was unfortunate, as nobody outside would be able to hear my screams of terror.

A familiar guy in track pants stopped me from entering. "Name?"

I raised an eyebrow. "Aaron, you know my name. I sit next to you in history."

Aaron waggled a clipboard at me. "Naaaame?" He dragged out the word, along with my patience, and I snatched the clipboard from him.

"Delilah James. Right here." I jabbed at it with my index finger. "And next time you want help with homework, I'm going to forget who *you* are."

I thrust the clipboard into his stomach, and he blinked, nonplussed. "Geez, Delilah. You don't have to be so mean. It's like you're already one of them."

"No, I'm not!" I jerked open the door and glanced over my shoulder. "And you should really rethink the track pants, since you don't even exercise your *brain*!"

Aaron hurled a rude name in my direction, but I'd already pressed on, fighting my way through a thick bunch of purple feather boas that dangled from the ceiling like a curtain of bad taste.

When I emerged, feathers plastered to my clothes and hair, I saw a girl sitting at a card table strewn with paper gift bags in every pastel color imaginable.

"Name?" the girl asked.

I was *not* about to play that game again.

"I'm just going to grab a seat." I pointed to a corner of the room crowded with folding chairs and girls pawing through gift bags.

"Fine." The girl shrugged. "That'll be twenty-five dollars."

I pressed my lips together. "Maybe I'll stand, then."

"It's not twenty-five dollars for the *chair*," the girl scoffed. "It's twenty-five dollars if you want to pledge the Debutantes."

"What?!" At that moment, the "indoor voice" sign didn't apply to me. "You want me to *pay* for this nightmare?"

Paige was at my side in two shakes of a ponytail. "It's okay, Jamie," she told the girl. "This one's taken care of."

Paige grabbed a mint-colored bag with my name on it and pulled me away, smiling at everyone all the while. "You *do* like to draw attention, don't you?" Her lips barely moved as she spoke through her teeth.

"You didn't mention a torture fee," I whispered.

Paige stopped and faced me, plucking a feather from my hair. "Delilah, I understand this is a difficult experience for you, but most of these girls are *proud* to be here."

I opened my mouth to answer, but Paige covered it with her hand.

"So," she continued, "if you could avoid using words like 'nightmare' and 'torture' and 'soulless creatures of darkness,' that would be great." Her eyes pleaded with mine for the briefest moment.

"All right." I took a deep breath and tried to relax. "What's in these bags, anyway?"

Paige smiled with relief. "As you know, the Debutantes are *the* most noticed student body group, and as such, we need to set a positive example." She grabbed my hands and forced them palm up as she removed a laminated card from the bag and held it up for my inspection. "This is a fashion card with all the brands you should and *shouldn't* wear, and . . . repeat after me." She held up one hand, as if taking an oath. "Getting caught in plaid is a travesty."

I stared at her. "I think you mean 'tragedy.'"

"Same difference."

"Actually—"

"New rule just for you." Paige jammed her hand in my face to silence me. "No correcting the president."

"Okay, okay." I backed up until I could see her palm without crossing my eyes.

Paige flipped open a compact that held small trays of eyeshadow and blush. "Now, this is a makeup set based on your skin season."

"My skin season?"

"You're an autumn," Paige said firmly. "Don't ever let anyone tell you different."

"Oookay." I watched her take out a lip gloss, tin of mints, tweezers, pop-out hairbrush, nail file, sparkly nail polish, and acne cream. "Is that it?"

"Not quite. The last, and probably most important thing you'll need, is this." She reached into the bag one final time and pulled out a purple whistle and chain.

"And this is for . . . ?"

Paige unraveled the chain and slipped it over my neck. "Protection against all evil outside the Debutantes. Blow on it three times, and the nearest Debutante will come running."

"What if I'm out in the middle of the woods?"

Paige frowned. "Debutantes don't go to the woods." She glanced at a clock on the wall. "It's almost time to start. Grab something from the refreshment table and take a seat." She nudged me in that direction, but I veered to the right when I spotted Ava picking over the desserts. She noticed me at the same moment and regarded me with a disdainful sniff.

"Attention! Attention, everyone!" Paige stood at a podium before the chairs, banging a gavel. "Could we please find seats and come to order?"

The largest game of musical chairs began as twenty-eight girls scrambled to find seats front and center. I chose one at the edge of the crowd, and Ava settled herself at the opposite end. As soon as every girl was seated, Paige cleared her throat.

"Welcome, pledges." She did a quick glance around the room. "I hope you enjoyed the refreshments and had a chance to inspect your Debutante gift bags." Her face took on a stern expression. "I expect you to put these items to good use."

In response I lifted the whistle and blew three loud tweets.

Paige flashed me an annoyed look. "The Debutante social is this Saturday night at the Brighton Country Club. You're expected to attend and dress appropriately. Nothing plain, and no school clothes."

She had just eliminated every item in my wardrobe.

"Your date must *also* be dressed appropriately and—"

I zoned out for the rest of the topic. Now I needed a dress *and* a date, and our mall didn't have a Build-a-Boyfriend store. I didn't dare glance at Ava, though I could sense her mocking laughter.

"Each of you will notice that you have something in common with *one* other person in this room." Paige held up a finger in case we couldn't count that high. "There are two student athletes, two members of the drama club, two members of the school newspaper, and so on."

Girls glanced around, trying to find their common denominator, and the volume in the room increased with each new pairing. Most of the pairs hugged each other and changed chairs so they could sit together, but Ava and I glared at each other across the room and didn't budge.

"Don't get too friendly," Paige warned. "Because *no* group will have both its members selected." She leaned against the podium and smiled. "You'll be competing against one another."

This brought a second wave of commotion, and I watched the other girls moan with despair or gasp in shock. I glanced at Ava, who appeared as passive as I felt. There could only be one lead reporter. We'd known that before we arrived.

Paige banged her gavel on the podium, and the girls quieted as the officers handed out manila folders.

"You'll each be receiving a Debutante packet that includes a red envelope." She gestured toward Friend 1, who was sifting through packets and searching for each girl. "Don't open it until I give the word. In each—"

"What's in the envelope?" someone asked.

Paige cast a sour glance at her, and I could tell she'd been planning a dramatic revelation.

"In each envelope," Paige continued, "will be the task you have to complete in order to become a full-fledged Debutante. On Saturday night you'll be expected to give a progress report."

As each girl accepted her manila folder, she removed the envelope and regarded it with an awed reverence. I received mine and used it to cover my mouth while I yawned.

When the officers finally stepped back from the crowd and nodded to Paige, she banged her gavel once, though there was no need. The room had fallen completely silent.

"Pledges"—she paused and smiled—"open your envelopes."

Chapter Six

The contents of my pledge envelope belonged in the hands of a secret agent, not a twelve-year-old reporter. Inside, a black-and-white photo had been clipped to a card with "Operation: Takedown" printed on it, along with my "Mission Objective." Hopefully I'd have a chance to read the instructions before the card self-destructed.

I glanced briefly at the photo of a bored-looking girl with short, pixie-ish hair, then moved on to the details of Operation Takedown.

Target: Katie Glenn, mastermind of Hot Stuff.

Overview: Katie transferred to Brighton Junior Academy in the spring semester of last year. Since her arrival, she's formed a small following of influential students that threatens the power dynamic of the Debutantes. She's been warned of this behavior but laughs at our efforts to make peace.

Mission Objective: Using your investigative journalism skills, uncover enough dirt on Katie to destroy her reputation and bring down Hot Stuff.

Deadline: One week from date of mission assignment.

With a frown I returned the card to its envelope and studied Katie's photo. This would definitely be a challenge. On the few occasions I'd spoken to Katie, she'd pointedly checked her watch to let me know how boring I was, and I only had one class with her, so eavesdropping would be difficult.

Although . . . she did tend to wander away from her desk a lot, leaving her binder easily accessible. Her locker was in the same bay as mine, *and* she probably had one or two members in Hot Stuff who loved to talk more than they should.

And, of course, investigative journalism was what I did best.

I leaned back in my chair and watched the other girls absorb their tasks. Some looked utterly terrified, as if they'd been asked to catch rabid monkeys. Ava, however, appeared as indifferent as usual. She studied her reflection in the Little Debbie compact and fanned herself with the pledge card. I couldn't help wishing she'd wave the paper more slowly so I could at least see the name of the mission. With the way my luck was going, her assignment was probably something simple like "Operation: Sing 'Frère Jacques'" or "Operation: Make Crepes."

At that moment, Ava glanced in my direction, snapped her compact shut, and grabbed her book bag. Before she could get Paige's attention, I hurried to my feet.

"Are we free to go?" I blurted. "I'd like to get started on my task right away."

Ava glared at me, but Paige beamed, no doubt appreciating my sudden change of heart. "Of course. The quicker you finish, the more dedicated you seem."

The other girls took one look at her approving smile and scrambled to gather their things, elbows flying as they raced one another to the door. Since I'd already received my enthusiasm points, I hung back from the insanity, as did Ava.

"You are pathetic," she whispered to me. "I will enjoy humiliating you." She puckered her lips as if she were about to spit in my face, thought better of it, and, with a dramatic flounce, disappeared through the curtain of feathers.

Someone else grabbed my arm, and I spun around with fists raised.

"Drop your weapons," said Paige, rolling her eyes. "I just wanted to give you this." She thrust my gift bag in my hands. "And I wanted to tell you that you'd better beat Ava. Otherwise, I'll look *so* lame for inviting you."

"Hmm. That *is* tempting." I shoved the gift bag into my pack. "But if you wanted me in the Little Debbies, you shouldn't have invited Ava."

Paige stepped closer and lowered her voice. "You think I had a choice? Even though they worship at my Louis V's, my officers still have minds of their own." She held up a finger. "Don't comment."

"I would never," I said, smiling.

"They want Ava because they don't see what a threat you are," she continued. "I have to prove them wrong, and I need *you* to do it."

Her conviction and foresight impressed me, even if her motive was purely selfish. "What's Ava's task?"

Paige glanced at the other Little Debbies lounging around the dessert table before answering. "She received the same assignment as you. Just a different clique—the Angels."

I snorted. "How can the Little Debbies already have two sets of enemies on the second day of school?"

Paige crossed her arms and raised an eyebrow. "I don't know, Delilah. Maybe you should check with Marcus and Renee."

My jaw dropped as I marveled at the clever comeback—and the fact that it had come from Paige. "Huh. Okay."

"Besides, Hot Stuff and the Angels aren't our enemies. They're our competition. Like Miss America."

"Yes, but the contestants in beauty pageants don't try to destroy one another."

Paige shook her head emphatically. "Not true. When I was in the Teen Dream competition, this horrible girl from Long Beach gave everyone 'good luck' cookies that she said were fat free." She paused for dramatic effect. "But they *weren't*."

"Fascinating." I shifted my backpack onto my shoulders. "I'll see you later."

"Try some of that blush tonight." She pantomimed with her hands. "But not too much or it'll clash with your hair and make you look like Ronald McDonald."

"Good-bye, Paige."

"And make friends with a pair of tweezers!" she called after me. "You're *this* close to having a unibrow!"

I pushed through the feathers and found the door. The brain trusts guarding it were gone, but to my dismay, Marcus was leaning against the building. As he fell into step beside me, I was astounded by my new talent to attract all manner of evil.

"We need to talk," he said.

"The Little Debbies gave me sanctuary, so you can't touch me," I reminded him.

"I said 'talk,' not fight."

"Okay." I pulled my cell out of my backpack and sent a text to Jenner. "So talk."

"You owe me an apology."

I snapped my phone shut and stared at him. "Not going to happen."

Marcus's face reddened, and his eyebrows formed a V of anger. "I had to change schools because of you, and you won't even say 'I'm sorry'?"

I frowned back. "*You're* the one who should apologize. To the entire school."

"I only dunked, like, ten people!"

"Yes, but you intimidated *everyone*," I said. "Kids were

terrified they might be next. The school counselor's schedule was booked solid for a month!"

Marcus's expression relaxed, and he looked a little pleased. "Really?"

I gave an exasperated groan. "Wrong answer. You should feel horrible for ruining people's lives!"

He stared at me, dumbfounded. "So should you. Instead, you're being welcomed into the popular crowd . . . all because of an article that made me look bad."

"Actually"—I cleared my throat—"because of an article that made the *Little Debbies* look bad."

"Whatever!" He waved his arms like a madman, a sign for me to start moving again.

"Good-bye." I quickened my pace toward the main building, and he matched me, stride for stride.

"Who are you going to exploit next?" His voice was close enough to my ear to startle me. "I mean, that *is* your pledge task, right?"

I swallowed and fixed my gaze ahead. "I don't know what you're talking about."

He laughed, but it was mirthless. "I'll bet you don't. I'll also bet that whoever you're about to destroy doesn't deserve it."

We reached the doors, and I jerked one of them open, pausing to look back at him. "Marcus, I'm sorry you did something stupid and got caught at it, but I'll never be sorry I told everyone." I was thankful to see Jenner waiting for me at one of the tables. "And since we talked about this now, I assume we won't have to talk tomorrow or ever again, so . . . have a nice life."

I nodded to Jenner, who scooped up an envelope sitting beside her and followed me down the hall.

"That's not really an apology!" called Marcus. "Crazy redhead!"

Jenner waited until we'd stepped off campus before saying, "I guess that's a 'no' on the follow-up interview?"

I sighed, relaxing my shoulders until they were no longer up by my ears. "*He* actually came looking for *me*. To get an apology because he had to change schools."

"Wow. Nothing like a little guilt before dinner."

I took the envelope from her and folded the flap back. Inside were pictures of various members of Hot Stuff she'd nabbed from the journalism room.

"Marcus left because he couldn't live with what he did," I said. "Not because of me."

"Well, it was a *little* because of you." As soon as she'd said the words, Jenner pointed to the envelope. "And before you smite me, remember that I busted my butt to run down here with these."

"Okay, okay." I pulled out the photos and flipped

through them slowly. Nothing jumped out at me. I hadn't really expected to see anything scandalous, but it would have been nice to see a picture of Katie shoplifting or kicking a puppy. "There's *nothing* unusual about Katie Glenn," I said with a sigh.

"Oh, yeah. *Nothing* unusual." Jenner leaned over my shoulder and smirked. "Unless you count her obsession with sea turtles, the fact that she only wears long-sleeve shirts, and her tendency to wander off mid-conversation."

"She does that to you, too? I thought I was the only one who drove her to boredom."

Jenner shook her head. "If you don't have a shell, you're lucky to get five minutes of her time."

"Note to self," I murmured. "Purchase turtle costume before talking to Katie." I held up a picture of her at a basketball game the previous school year. "Her hair was really short back then. Shorter than it is now."

"Well, it *does* grow."

I gave Jenner a withering glance. "That's not what I mean. She hasn't worn it that short ever since. Why not?"

Jenner shrugged. "Because she realized it made her look like a guy? Who knows." She took the picture and fanned herself with it. "What exactly did the Little Debbies ask you to do to Katie, anyway?" The disapproving tone I'd been waiting for finally worked its way into her voice.

"They want me to bring down her clique, which involves digging up dirt on her officers."

"Oh." Jenner's tone changed to one of surprise. "So, you're just writing an exposé on another clique."

I nodded. "Nothing's changed. I'm still the same girl doing the same things."

Jenner nodded. "While wearing a hideous purple whistle." She pointed to my neck and I blushed.

"It's supposed to be my personal security system." I tucked the whistle under my shirt. "When I blow on it, mermaids swim to my rescue or something."

"Not a bad idea, given your situation," she said. "You should definitely wear it to the beach tonight."

I stared at her as if she were speaking a different language. "The beach?"

Jenner gasped in mock surprise. "Don't tell me the Little Debbies aren't in the know!"

I pushed her. "Paige is allergic to seaweed, so she doesn't care about the beach. Why? What's happening there?"

"Twilight Surf." Jenner leaned forward conspiratorially. "And rumor has it that a certain editor and his new girlfriend will be there *and* there may be a few sea turtles as well."

"Really." My fingers curled around the edges of the pictures. "How interesting."

Chapter Seven

As I rummaged through my closet for Twilight Surf clothes, I gave serious thought to blowing my whistle. On the list of Little Debbie emergency situations, I was certain that fashion crises ranked somewhere between breakups and bad facials.

Even though I owned enough khaki to outfit a preppy army, my wardrobe suffered from a severe lack of sundresses, skirts, or anything remotely feminine. Nobody, in my opinion, would take a reporter in a halter top seriously.

After waffling between a dress with a lace collar and a skirt covered in smiling ladybugs, I chose the lesser of the two embarrassments and slipped into the dress.

When I strolled into the kitchen, Major had his head buried in the refrigerator, so I tapped him on the shoulder.

"Bye, Major! I'll be back after dinner."

I managed three steps toward the door before I heard him say, "Hold up there, Delilah."

I scowled at the ceiling before turning around. "Yes?"

Major stood "at ease," legs apart and arms folded behind his back. "You're wearing one of your old dresses."

I glanced down as if noticing it for the first time. "Yes."

"To the beach."

My weight shifted from one foot to the other. "Yes."

Major leaned forward and, in a voice barely above a whisper, asked, "Why?"

"Because . . ." My hands went to the lace collar, which now felt like a noose. "Most girls . . . I mean, this guy . . ."

From the look on Major's face, I knew there was no right answer.

"Delilah," he said. "I don't like the idea of you changing yourself for *anybody*." He frowned. "Especially if it means you'll be dressing like an urban pilgrim."

"Pilgrims don't wear sneakers," I pointed out.

Major turned me to face my bedroom. "Into your normal clothes, please."

Fifteen minutes later, I was stepping onto a city bus with Jenner, wearing khaki shorts and a polo shirt.

"You look nice," she said. "That outfit is very you."

"But it's the me Ben already knows," I countered. "The simple Delilah who threw up in his living room. I want him to see a more sophisticated Delilah."

Jenner blinked at me. "You're twelve. Sophisticated doesn't happen until college."

I regarded my reflection in the bus window. "Ava's sophisticated."

"Blah. Ava's an alien from the planet Pretentious." She dug into her beach bag and pulled out a magazine and a pack of licorice.

"What's this about?" I took the magazine from her.

It was the same issue Paige had shown me the day before but with some of the pages marked by scraps of paper. "You *never* read these kinds of magazines."

"My mom got me a subscription over the summer." She snapped a licorice whip in half with her teeth. "And I found some articles that made me think of you."

I flipped through the marked pages, reading the headlines.

PEER PRESSURE: THE PERSONALITY KILLER.

THE GOOD GIRL'S GUIDE TO GETTING WHAT YOU WANT.

SQUASHING THE JEALOUSY BUG.

I lowered the magazine and fixed Jenner with a steely gaze. "What a *thoughtful* friend you are."

She sighed. "I'm just looking out for you."

"No, you're pointing out what *you* think is wrong with me!" The bus driver glanced at us in the mirror, and I lowered my voice. "*None* of these articles apply. I mean, they're even more irrelevant than *this*." I jabbed at an article entitled "The 411 on Flirting."

"Fine." Jenner focused all her attention on shredding her licorice into strands. "Sorry."

Seeing the embarrassed look on her face, I wilted. "No, I'm sorry. You're just trying to help."

She nodded. "I want you to beat Ava, but I don't want you to forget about the *real* reason you're doing it."

I gave her a questioning look, and she rolled her eyes. "The *newspaper*!"

"Right! No, I won't," I promised. "In fact, I'm going to interview Katie while I'm there and see if I can learn more about Hot Stuff."

"Good!" She smiled and returned her attention to a novel that had a decapitated princess on the cover.

To humor Jenner, I decided to read one of the articles she'd marked for me . . . until my eyes were drawn to the opposite page blasting the 411 on flirting.

It was laid out like a comic strip, featuring a girl shooting a heart-shaped arrow at a boy. They didn't look a thing like me or Ben—but that didn't stop me from making the comparison. When I glanced at the rules for flirting, they seemed simple and straightforward:

1. Be approachable. Flip that hair, show those pearly whites, and laugh it up. Guys love girls who know how to have fun.

2. Maintain eye contact. Guys want to know you're focused on them and *only* them.

3. Compliment, compliment, compliment! Flattery will get you everywhere.

4. Actions speak louder than words. Touch his arm and create that personal connection to let him know you're interested.

5. Be his mirror so that your body language matches his. Imitation is the sincerest form of flattery, and, as we all know, flattery will get you everywhere.

Jenner bumped my elbow. "Come on. This is our stop."

I closed the magazine before I reached the end of the comic, but I knew the girl had won the heart of the boy. And if a one-dimensional scribble could get what she was after, it couldn't be *that* difficult for me, could it?

Jenner and I grabbed our beach bags and trudged toward a big painted banner that read TWILIGHT SURF in sickly green letters. Once the sun went down, the paint would make the words glow in the dark, like miniature moons.

Twilight Surf was the annual opportunity for the seventh graders at Brighton to mingle with the students from their next stage of learning, Woodcliff Finishing School. Naturally, there was a surfing competition, but there were also bonfires, barbecues, and plenty of chances to be seen. Several girls had already set up their beach gear near the lifeguard stand where the Woodcliff guys hung out.

"Where should we go?" I asked Jenner.

"Well, I have to sign in for the competition first." She pointed to her parents' surf shop, Jenner's Bay, where a line of teenage guys and girls flowed out the door and onto the sand. "Do you want to come with me?"

I slid on my sunglasses to block the last rays of light and glanced around. "I think I'm going to see if I can find Katie."

Jenner nodded. "Head toward the shore. She'll probably be camped out there, waiting for turtles."

We separated and I picked my way down the rocky slope toward the sand, checking each group of girls I passed for one with short, punky hair.

And then I saw *her.*

Ava, in *another* strapless dress, was chatting up a group of girls all wearing the same T-shirt with a large pair of wings patterned on the back. She looked infuriatingly pretty with her dark hair pulled into a messy bun and her French sophistication oozing out of every pore of her body. The other girls wore flip-flops, but Ava wore high-heeled sandals. Their beach towels were simple, funky colors, but Ava's had a massive print of the Eiffel Tower.

Slowly and quietly, I lowered my bag to the ground and opened it to grab my towel. Neither Ava nor the Angels had noticed me yet, and if I set up a towel behind them, I could probably hear their entire conversation and learn Ava's plan of attack.

It would have worked, except my phone chose to blast its ringtone at that moment. I turned my back to the girls before they could see me and grabbed my things, walking toward Jenner's Bay as fast as I could. "Hello?" I whispered into the phone before Ava could discover the identity of her seaside stalker.

"Delilah?" At the sound of Ben's voice, I almost did a face plant in the sand.

"Ben! Hi!" The volume of my voice shot way past normal; I cringed and cleared my throat. "I mean . . . what's up?"

"Ava's following some story lead, so I'm hanging out at

Jenner's Bay. Did you want to grab a soda while I wait for her to get back?"

I would have turned cartwheels if my hands hadn't been full . . . and if I'd had some athletic talent. "Sure! I'm on my way now."

I squeezed past the crowd on the shop steps and headed for the porch, where my heart momentarily stalled. Ben was leaning against the railing, looking out at the ocean. The sun highlighted his profile like a golden aura of gorgeous.

"Hey!" He reached behind him and produced two glass bottles of cola with straws. "You still like these, right?"

Old-fashioned soda was my favorite, and my skin prickled with goose bumps, knowing Ben had thought of me.

"Amazing memory," I said, taking a big swallow.

Ben smiled even broader, and at that moment, I realized the magazine had been right. I'd paid a guy a compliment, and he'd been flattered!

I, Delilah James, was officially flirting.

With renewed confidence I smiled at Ben and flipped my hair over my shoulder. "I like your shirt, too. It . . . fits you well."

"Thanks." He looked down at himself. "I guess Ava's pretty good at choosing sizes."

My right eye twitched at the mention of her name *and* the

fact that she was dressing him, but I flipped my hair again and kept smiling.

"I'm glad you're not still upset about the newspaper thing." He studied my eyes, and I stared into his, unblinking.

"You're the editor," I said, still grinning while I sipped from my straw. My cheeks were beginning to hurt from so much smiling. "You know what's best." I did another hair flip.

Ben leaned away from me, and I leaned away from him, still maintaining eye contact and a winning smile. "Are you okay?" His eyes narrowed a bit while he studied me.

I nodded and tried to touch his arm, which was difficult to do with both of us leaning away. In the end, I swatted at his wrist with my fingertips. "Of course!" I laughed heartily to prove my point, but Ben didn't join in.

"What did they put in this?" He grabbed my soda bottle.

"Ha! You are *so* funny!" I patted his back harder than I intended as he brought the bottle up to sniff it.

Until that moment, I'd never known how far a straw could go up a boy's nose.

"Oh, my gosh!" I could barely form the words, my jaw was so stiff from smiling. "I'm really sorry!" I tried to help him, but Ben turned his back to me and waved a dismissive hand.

"It's okay. I've got it."

I hovered behind him, glancing over my shoulder to see how many people had witnessed my failed flirting. Judging from the stares and whispers, I guessed all of them.

A second later, Ben turned back around, straw in hand, rubbing his nose. "Ta-da!" He faced the crowd, who clapped appreciatively. "Thank you. For my next trick, I'll pull a French fry out of my ear."

Everyone laughed, except me, and Ben nudged my side. "Oh, come on. After what you just did to me, I at least deserve a smile."

The guy was cute, funny, and sweet. At his request, I'd stick a straw up my *own* nose. Plus, it *was* pretty amusing. So, I grinned.

"No offense, but I don't think I want that straw back."

He laughed and I joined in, but our fun was cut short by a voice hissing in my ear.

"I appear to have missed something very funny."

Ben stepped away from me and placed the sodas on the railing. "Hey, Ava! That was quick."

She swept past to stand between us, an arm curled around Ben's neck. "You seem to have had a more interesting time than I did."

"Nah," said Ben. "Just a little accident." He pointed to his nose, and Ava cooed and clicked her tongue.

"What did that wicked girl do to you?" She held his face in her hands and kissed his nose.

I turned away, not wanting to see if he had kissed her back. "Well, thanks for keeping me company, Ben. I'm going to go find Jenner."

Ben disentangled himself from Ava. "Come find us later, okay?" And then he was smothered again by 115 pounds of French pretension.

"Sure." I pulled open the door to the shop. "Later."

Jenner waited just inside, pointing out one of the huge windows overlooking the beach . . . and the spot where Ben and I had been standing. "*What* was that?"

I sighed and leaned against the glass, crumpling to the floor. "I don't know. I was just doing what the magazine article said."

Jenner crouched beside me. "Which one told you to laugh like a crazy person and avoid blinking entirely?"

I gave her a pained look. "The 411 on flirting."

Jenner sighed and patted the top of my head. "Poor, naive Delilah. Those articles are written by thirty-year-old women who share dinner conversation with their cats. They know *nothing* about romance."

"I'm not in a romance. I've definitely made sure of that." My phone rang again and I stood to answer it. "Hello?"

"*What* have you been doing?" Paige's nasal voice pierced

my eardrum. "You're supposed to be working on your pledge task."

I rolled my eyes at Jenner and mouthed Paige's name. "I am," I said into the phone. "I'm at Twilight Surf looking for Hot Stuff right now."

"No, you're not!" was Paige's indignant reply. "You're at Jenner's Bay embarrassing yourself."

Chapter Eight

I stared at the phone as if Paige were crawling through the earpiece. "How do you know that?"

"I can see you," said Paige. "And by the way, you're a terrible flirt."

"You're spying on me?" I asked in disbelief.

I crouched down, pulling Jenner with me. A quick glance around the shop revealed not a single feather, sequin, or piece of glitter to give away Paige's location. "Where are you?"

"In the bungalows by the board-walk."

I lifted my head to peek over the window ledge and saw Ava and Ben still cuddling on the patio. Beyond them, I could see the beach huts, including one with a girl holding a cell phone and pair of binoculars. "You look like a stalker."

"I've got to keep an eye on my interests."

"Do you do this to all the pledges?"

"Just the ones I've placed bets on."

I brought my palm to my face and tried to massage away the irritation. "*What* are you talking about?"

"One of my officers bet Juicy that you'd lose."

I shook my head in confusion. "Who's Juicy?"

Paige exhaled a long-suffering sigh. "Let me rephrase for the fashion-impaired who have not bothered to read their fashion cards. One of my officers bet her Juicy Couture *hoodie* that you would lose."

"So, you're spying on me to win someone's used gym clothes." I winked at Jenner. "That seems beneath you, Paige."

A loud banging issued from the other end of the receiver, and I could see Paige smacking her phone against the window sill. "Not funny, Delilah!"

"Okay, okay! Quit abusing your cell."

Paige placed the phone back against her ear. "You should be thanking me instead of teasing me. I've already found Katie for you."

I snapped up straight. "Why didn't you say so? Where is she?"

"Maybe I won't tell," Paige said with a hint of a pout. "Maybe I'll make you find her on your own."

I knew she wanted me to beg, but I wasn't about to give in.

"That's fine," I said. "Because if I don't find her, you'll lose your bet . . . and your pride."

Silence greeted me on the other end of the line, but I could hear Paige breathing into the phone. I glanced out the window, where I could see her watching me, arms crossed.

"Fine," she said flatly. "Katie's down at the main bonfire."

"Thank you."

"And take someone else to the social on Saturday. Ben's lame!"

The line went dead, and Paige closed the curtains of her window with a vicious jerk.

I returned the phone to my pocket and turned to Jenner, who just shook her head. "You know this whole situation is insane and *so* not worth it."

Her judgmental look had returned, soon to be followed by a talk about being true to myself. "Is it really any different than what you're doing?" I gestured to the line of surfers. "I'm competing for a title, and you're competing for a title. Which, by the way, is happening *when*?"

It was *the* most obvious change of subject but the easiest way to drop the issue.

Jenner hesitated and frowned before finally answering, "I'm going at six-thirty. You have half an hour."

I squeezed her shoulders and sprinted out of the shop, pushing past Ben and Ava as they stepped onto the beach. As I got closer to the bonfire, I slowed my pace and smoothed my clothes. So far nobody had commented on my lack of appropriate beach attire, but the entire group gathered there wore nothing more formal than bathing suits. Compared to them, I might as well have been wearing an evening gown.

Around the bonfire the cliques separated themselves with barriers of boys. I spotted Katie and several Hot Stuff girls wedged between a few jocks on one side and a few smotties on the other.

"I'm just soooo busy with parties and new members and NFP," I heard her saying. "My social calendar is *full* until November."

"Hi, Katie?" I lowered myself to the sand beside her. My rule of approaching divas was the same as my rule for approaching strange dogs—always stay at their eye level. Divas hated for anyone to tower above them.

Katie half glanced in my direction, annoyed at the interruption. "Do I know you?"

"Delilah James." I held out my hand. "Lead reporter for the *Brighton Bugle*."

She didn't so much as wag a pinky in my direction. "I thought Ava Piquet was the lead reporter."

My fists clenched involuntarily and I hid them behind my back. "We're . . . sharing the position, actually."

Katie said nothing as she kicked sand onto the fire, which hissed and receded.

"So," I said, "I was hoping you might be interested in doing an interview for the school paper?"

Katie glanced at the girl to her right. "What's our current media coverage?"

The girl made a thumbs-down. "Nonexistent."

From the way Katie jerked off her sunglasses, I knew it wasn't the answer she'd been expecting. "One of the new girls says her father works for Channel 5! Why are we not taking advantage of that?"

"Um . . . it could have to do with the fact that his job at the station is to mop floors and clean toilets."

"Oooooh!" Katie squeezed handfuls of sand in her fist and threw them down. "Send her a note of dismissal tomorrow morning. *Nobody* tricks me and gets away with it."

I cleared my throat, both to remind Katie I was still there *and* to fight off a laugh. "If you'd like, I can interview Hot Stuff as a group."

Katie pushed her sunglasses onto the top of her head like a makeshift headband and looked at me as if seeing me for the first time. "You're the girl who wrote the article bashing the Debutantes last year."

"Yeah, she is," said someone in the group of jocks. A couple of them shifted over, and Marcus leaned toward us. "She also wrote a great article about me." He smiled cruelly. "Didn't you?"

I groaned in exasperation. "Marcus! Isn't your parole officer looking for you?"

A chorus of "Oooh"s and laughter punctuated the crackling of the bonfire.

Instead of getting angry, Marcus scooted closer. "You know, if anyone had one, it—"

"I'm hungry," Katie announced, getting to her feet. "I'm going to buy a hot dog, Dana. Come with me."

When she sauntered off alone, I realized she'd been talking to me. I stuck my tongue out at Marcus and hurried after Katie. "Listen—"

"Don't"—Katie held up a hand—"give me commands."

I took a steadying breath. "Okay. About that article—"

"I hate the Debutantes," she said. "So, hooray for you."

"Oh, good!"

"That's why I'm giving you from the time it takes for me to get to the stand and back to ask questions."

By those terms, I had about five minutes, but it was better than nothing. I slid a spiral notepad out of my back pocket.

"I'd like to start by learning a little more about you."

Katie froze, one foot on the boardwalk. "Me?" She turned in my direction. "Why me?"

"Because . . . you're the leader of Hot Stuff," I said. "People are always interested in the person who makes a group tick." I watched her face closely. Her eyebrows furrowed a bit and her cheeks appeared pinched, not to mention the sweat on her forehead. This was definitely a girl with something to hide.

"Well, I'd rather not give you anything *too* personal about me," she said, walking again. "Our group needs to maintain some anonymity."

"Fair enough," I said. "Where did you go to school before this?"

The question was fairly simple and straightforward, but Katie stumbled a bit on the smooth stone surface of the boardwalk.

"Before this?" she repeated. "I went to . . . Fowler. Hot tonight, isn't it?" She dabbed at her forehead but made no motion to roll up her sleeves.

"Not if you wear a T-shirt," I said casually. "What made you decide to change schools?"

"I *never* wear T-shirts." Katie fished around in her pocket for money. "And my dad got transferred."

I frowned. "But Fowler is only a few blocks from here.

Why wouldn't you just stay until you graduated?"

She shrugged. "It was time for a change of scenery."

I lowered my notepad and fixed my eyes on hers. "But . . . don't you miss your friends?"

Katie snorted. "Please, they're only a few blocks away. I see them all the time."

We stopped at the back of the line for the hot dog stand. "Were you in charge of a clique at your old school?" I asked.

Katie tilted her head to one side and smiled. "Yeah. You could say that."

I drew several circles around the name of her school.

"What activities are you involved in besides Hot Stuff? I heard you mentioning NFP. What's that?"

Again, Katie hesitated. "That's just an awareness group I belong to. We . . . raise awareness."

I blinked at her and made a note to research NFP. "What makes you such a natural-born leader?" I returned to my questioning.

"Well," she chewed on her lip and squinted in concentration. "I refuse to give up until I get my way."

My pen paused on the page. That wasn't a qualification for a leader; it was the qualification for Spoiled Brat of the Year. "Um . . . what else?"

"Let's see . . ." She placed her food order and drummed her fingers on the counter. "Oh! I'm compassionate."

A giggle escaped, but I turned it into a cough. "How so?"

"I saved a sea turtle."

"Interesting." I wrote some more. "How?"

"Duh. By rescuing it."

I pressed my lips together. "From what?"

"Danger."

My pen pressed a hole through the paper. "What *kind* of danger?"

Katie looked as annoyed as I felt. "Life-threatening."

"*Fine.* Why the name Hot Stuff?"

"Because we're hot stuff."

I put down my pen and smiled at her. "These answers explain a lot and aren't at *all* vague. Thank you."

Not surprisingly, she didn't quite catch my sarcasm. "You're welcome."

The vendor handed her a hot dog and I tried for another question. "How do you decide who gets to be Hot Stuff?"

"Oh." Katie hid her mouth behind her hand and talked while she chewed. "We avoid deviants or social outcasts. Only the best of the best." She gripped my arm. "But we *don't* discriminate against nerds, fat girls, or trailer trash." She pointed at my notepad. "Make sure you put that. That's important."

"Oh, definitely," I said in a serious voice. "Everyone needs to know what humanitarians you are."

Katie paused in her chewing and looked thoughtful.

"You know, I never thought of it that way, but you're right. We're like Mother Teresa—only younger and cuter."

She started walking toward the beach again, and I rolled my eyes behind her back. I asked her a few more general questions to keep her from getting suspicious, and when she reached the bonfire again, she turned to me and extended a hand.

"Dana, it was nice talking to you. Why don't we discuss the article some more tomorrow at school?"

I couldn't resist a genuine smile. The leader of Hot Stuff felt comfortable enough around me for a second round of interview questions. Eventually, if I wheedled and flattered enough, she'd let down her guard, and I'd get all the information I needed. "Thanks, Katie. That would be great."

I shook her hand, the watch on my wrist reminding me that I only had a few minutes before Jenner's turn at the tide.

Bidding Katie a quick farewell, I hurried down the beach and jumped several sand castles and people to reach the shore just as Jenner was paddling out to catch her first wave. Her dad stood by the judge's table, so I joined him and dropped to the sand to catch my breath.

"How's the competition?"

He scratched his beard. "It's tough. Jenner decided to go against the older group, where the surfers are *much* fiercer."

We watched Jenner jump to her feet and catch an impressive wave into shore, only wobbling a bit on the dismount. I cheered, and her father whistled through his teeth.

"She might have a fighting chance," he said.

I looked up at him to agree, but a broad-shouldered figure caught my eye. Marcus was slogging toward me, taking the exact path I'd run to the shore.

"Marcus, are you *following* me?" Despite my irritation, I couldn't help feeling a little flattered. Most reporters didn't get their own personal stalkers until they'd reached the national news circuit.

Jenner's dad glanced over at us, frowning. "Everything okay, Delilah?"

"Yes," I said, "just some guy from school."

"We're working on a project together," Marcus told Jenner's dad.

"I see." He nodded at Marcus but didn't take his eyes off him.

I grabbed Marcus's arm and jerked him down to my level. "I thought I was done dealing with you!" My whisper was harsh enough to cause Jenner's dad to look down.

Marcus nodded and smiled for his benefit. "I just came to offer what we both know you want."

I snorted and waved a dismissive hand. "You have *nothing* I want."

"Not even a follow-up article to"—he leaned forward—"the Swirlie Bandit?"

My eyes widened, but I tried to keep my cool. "Maybe . . ."

Marcus smirked and settled back on his elbows. "I realize you'll never give me an outright apology, so instead, I want you to give me an interview . . . a chance to tell my side of the story."

I studied his face to see if he was serious. "You realize since I'm writing the article, you can't make up things that didn't happen. I'd just leave them out."

He nodded. "I also know you're obsessed with the truth, and even if it makes me look *better*, you'll still tell it."

When I didn't say anything, he continued. "Look, there's no catch to any of this. I just want a chance for people to see me *not* as this jerk you invented."

"But you *are* a jerk," I countered.

He shrugged. "If you don't want the article, I can think of another person who'll take it and completely debunk the article you wrote about me."

My eyes narrowed. "Ava." Somehow she always managed to force her French fanny into my life.

"Yep," said Marcus. "Personally I think I'm being generous, coming to *you* first with the offer."

I almost objected again, but a sneaky plan had started to formulate in my mind. "Okay," I said slowly. "I *will* interview you."

"Good."

"Saturday night."

"Fine."

"At the Debutante social."

Marcus leaned forward, looking far less smug. "Huh?"

"I need a date," I said simply. "And you're available."

He laughed but didn't sound amused. More like . . . incredulous. "We"—he gestured emphatically between me and himself—"don't get along. Why would I possibly agree to that?"

"Some of the most influential kids in school will be there, and if you want to improve your reputation . . ." I let the idea dangle in front of him.

Of course, I was mostly lying. His bad-boy reputation would always precede him, even if he showed up at the country club in a tuxedo and top hat. The real reason I wanted to bring him was to horrify the Little Debbies with his presence. If I was stuck pledging, I might as well have fun messing with them.

I watched Marcus and could almost hear the rusty gears struggling to turn in his brain. The way he squinted at me, I knew he didn't believe everything I'd said, but the fact that he was still quiet meant he thought I had a point.

After a moment of listening to the waves and cheering crowd, he finally nodded. "All right. I'll let you interview me at the social. But it's strictly professional. We're *not* holding hands and you're *not* going to call me your date or your boyfriend or anything sweet."

I smiled. "Don't worry. I can think of *plenty* of things to call you that aren't sweet at all."

"Just give me the details."

I did, but I left out the dress code. I was curious to see what he'd come up with on his own.

When I finished, he jumped to his feet, brushing off his shorts and deliberately flicking sand at me. "I'll pick you up at seven, then." He ran off before I could shout, "It's a date!"

Jenner and her dad were standing near the judge's table waiting for her results, so I got up to join them, only to find Ava barring my path.

"Ava." I pasted on my biggest, fakest smile. "What an unpleasant surprise."

"That was exactly what *I* thought," she said with a sneer, "when I saw you throwing yourself at Benjamin."

"Throwing?" My eyebrows rose, knocking some of Marcus's discarded sand into my eyes. "*He* called and invited *me* to join him."

Ava's constant look of supremacy faltered, but a second later, her face was a stone wall. "He must have felt sorry for you, wandering on the beach, dressed like that." She gestured scornfully at my outfit. "But I did not come to point out the obvious. I came to give you a warning."

I smiled and crossed my arms. "What's the warning, Ava?"

She threw her hair over one shoulder and stepped forward until her nose touched mine. "Stay away from Benjamin or I will make your life . . . *impossible*!"

I sputtered a laugh and accidentally sent spit flying into her face. Ava squealed and pawed at her cheeks as if she'd been struck with acid, and I laughed even harder.

"You can't even handle a little saliva. How are you going to make good on your threat?"

Ava glowered at me through her fingertips. "I assure you. You do not want to find out."

Chapter Nine

I swung out of bed Friday morning and headed to the kitchen with an extra bounce of confidence. In one night I'd made Ava jealous, secured Katie's confidence, and gotten a date for the Debutante social. On top of *that*, I had a great story for the first edition that wouldn't involve frogs or garbage-eating students.

As long as Marcus came through on his offer, of course.

"You're in good spirits." Major pushed a plate of breakfast in front of me. "Did you resolve that issue with the French girl?"

I smiled and downed a forkful of

egg. "Nope. She's actually grown to loathe me." I beamed. "Apparently, *I've* become a threat to *her*."

"Well, that's outstanding!" Major clapped me on the shoulder. "Not the loathing part, of course, but it's nice to see you holding your own." He settled into the chair opposite mine. "Did you learn all about her, like I suggested?"

"Well, not *all* about her." I drank some orange juice. "Enough."

"Which is . . . ?"

I shrugged. "Her awards, where she's from . . . stuff like that."

Major folded his arms in front of him. "Delilah, that's *not* enough. If she takes the newspaper as seriously as you do *and* she now considers you a threat, you could be looking at all-out warfare."

I rolled my eyes. "This isn't the military, Major. Don't be so dramatic."

"I'm serious. You may not be talking tanks and ICBMs, but if she dislikes you as much as you think, she'll try to keep you from your objective."

I remembered Ava's threat to me on the beach and laughed. "You mean she'll try to make my life . . . *impossible*?"

"If there's one thing I've learned from taking care of an almost-teenage girl"—Major pushed himself up from the chair—"it's that they're very fond of the word 'impossible.'"

* * *

My first task of the day was chatting up Katie to see if she was ready to spill all her deepest, darkest secrets. I dropped my books at my locker and avoided the menacing sneer of Renee Mercer, who was trying to hide her linebacker body behind a foot-wide pole.

Summoning my best smile, I walked confidently up to Katie and her entourage.

"Hey, Katie!" I nodded to the others. "Girls."

An uncomfortable silence followed, and I felt a momentary déjà vu as Katie lifted her gaze slightly in my direction before continuing to talk to her friends.

On the off-chance that she'd already forgotten who I was, I said, "I'm Delilah James. We talked last night about me interviewing you for the paper?"

A gum-cracking girl with a poodle perm nudged one of my shoulders with her fingertips, pushing me away. "We *all* know who you are, and you're not welcome here." She gestured to the space surrounding her.

I ignored the girl and maneuvered closer to Katie. "Sorry. Did I miss something important while I was sleeping?"

Katie snapped her fingers and Poodle Perm thrust a newspaper in my face. I recognized it as the piece I'd written on the Little Debbies.

"Okay," I said, "but we already talked about this, remember? I'm not writing another piece like this about *you*."

Katie glowered at me. "Save it, Nosy Newsie. Ava told me what you're up to."

My vocabulary suddenly became a caveman's. "Wha . . . uh . . ."

Ava had ratted me out. The Little Debbies hadn't said the pledge tasks were top secret, but I'd assumed everyone would keep quiet on an honor system. Still, I had to respond to the accusation, so I opted for the time-honored reply of all guilty parties.

"What are you talking about?"

The girls of Hot Stuff snorted like a herd of angry bulls.

"You want to be one of *them*." Poodle Perm jabbed at the Little Debbies article. "And they want you to make us look bad."

I didn't know what to say. From the looks on their faces, Hot Stuff already knew what they wanted to believe. The best I could do was offer up a smile to Katie and say, "Well, if you change your mind, let me know."

"I wouldn't hold my breath if I were you." Katie smirked, and Hot Stuff laughed rudely.

There was nothing left for me to do but walk away, my cheeks burning with embarrassment. I found Jenner at her locker and mimed bashing my head with the door.

"You know, it's more effective if you actually *let* it hit you," she said, smiling.

"I can't believe she did this!" I blurted.

"Who?" Jenner tossed her lunch bag into her locker. "Paige, Ava, or Katie?"

"Ava! Last night she threatened to ruin my life if I talked to Ben, and this morning she tells Katie and the Hot Stuff about my pledge task to destroy them!"

My phone buzzed in my backpack, and I flipped it open to read a text message.

You've been compromised. Paige

"How does she find out these things so fast?" I snapped it shut.

"Who?" Jenner closed her locker door. "Paige, Ava, or Katie?"

"Paige! It's like she has cameras all over the school." I glanced at the ceiling suspiciously. "And I haven't even talked to Ben again! She completely jumped the gun."

Jenner groaned and shook me by the shoulders. "*Who?* Paige, Ava, or Katie?"

"Ava!" I could have kicked myself for laughing off the warnings. Instead, I kicked the floor.

"Look, go talk to the Angels and tell them what Ava's up to," said Jenner. "Give her a taste of her own medicine."

"No, I can't copy her. That's weak." I jerked the Little

Debbies whistle out from under my shirt and waved it at Jenner. "But I could blow on this!"

"And how could the Little Debbies possibly help in this situation?" Jenner crossed her arms. "Other than telling you to stop frowning or you'll get wrinkles."

"Maybe when they learn she's being underhanded, they'll automatically disqualify her!" My eyes brightened as I hammered out a text to Paige. "Then I'll get the clique spot, all the best articles, and the lead reporter position, *and* Ben will realize what a mistake he's making with Ava!"

"Stop!" Jenner smacked me on the forehead and snatched away the phone. "You are one step away from being fitted for a straitjacket."

I closed my eyes and took a deep breath. "You're right. I've got to stay calm."

"And you've got to quit focusing on *yourself* and congratulate your best friend."

I opened my eyes. "For what?"

Jenner bounced up and down, a huge grin on her face. "I got invited to a surf competition in Malibu!" She produced a letter from her pocket that opened with "Congratulations!"

"Jenner!" I took the letter and hugged her. "How awesome. Did you just get this?"

She nodded. "Last night. After you left, this older guy came up to me while I was rinsing off my board. At first,

I thought he might be holding a knife so he could cut off my fingers and wear them around his neck, because he looked kind of crazy"—she took a breath—"but then as he got closer, I recognized him as the guy who owns Big Stick surfboards. He started talking to me and said he'd never seen a girl do so well in the boys' league."

"You were in the boys' league?" I squeaked. "That is beyond amazing!"

"Thank you." She bowed at the waist. "Anyway, he's one of the main sponsors for this invitation-only competition, and he got me into the junior division, so not this weekend but next, I'm going to be hanging with the big dogs in Malibu-u!" She sang the last words and did an impromptu dance.

"You know . . ." I chewed my lip thoughtfully. "That could make a great story for the newspaper. Students who break gender and age boundaries to compete in sports." I pointed at her. "You could be my feature interview."

She waved me away modestly. "No."

"Yes!" I snapped my fingers. "I'm going to pitch both the Marcus article and your article to run next Monday." I smiled and gazed into the distance.

Ava would have one vague piece about a shoplifter she couldn't even identify, while I'd be showcasing girls in a positive light *and* following up on the open-ended story of the Swirlie Bandit's fall from power.

"It's all coming together," I murmured.

Jenner stared blankly at me. "Did I not smack you hard enough? You've got a crazy look in your eye again."

"I'm fine," I said.

But I was more than fine. Taking Marcus to the Debutante social was a good scheme, but an even grander scheme was waiting for my execution, and I had precious little time.

"I'll see you in journalism," I told her, smiling. "And bring your own popcorn. It's going to be quite a show."

By the time I'd reached the journalism room, everyone was seated and watching Ben write on the dry erase board. Jenner pulled her book bag out of a chair next to her.

"I expected you to come in juggling poodles. Where's the show?"

I grinned and held up a page I'd ripped from my spiral notepad. "It's a seven-man show."

Jenner regarded me curiously, but I folded my hands in my lap and leaned back in my chair, staring at Ava.

When she noticed me, she smiled, catlike, and stretched her arms luxuriously in front of her, cracking her fingers at the finish. I smiled back and added a little wink.

Instantly Ava frowned, eyebrows furrowing and hands slinking back so she could drum her fingertips against her chin. It wasn't often that I got the chance to unnerve some-one, but when I did, it felt like Christmas.

Ben turned to face the room. "Okay, here's what we have lined up for next week." He tapped the board. "Any last-minute suggestions?"

I raised my hand. "I'm dropping my article on desper-ate dating"—several people giggled—"for one on breaking gender rules, with Jenner as my interviewee."

Jenner blushed but looked pleased.

"I like that *much* better." Ben nodded and grabbed for an eraser.

"I'm also doing a *second* article that's a follow-up to an earlier piece," I continued.

"Which one?" asked Ben, scribbling on the board.

"The Swirlie Bandit."

Ben's marker squeaked to a halt. "Really."

I nodded. "He wants to tell his version of the story."

"*His* version of the story." Ben snorted derisively.

I'd expected a negative response from him, but I didn't expect such a look of loathing. "And is there a reason you want to waste your time listening to his lies?"

I stared at Ben, mystified. "Do you not want me to write this piece?" It was a bad time to find out, especially since Marcus would be at the same social Ben was attending.

"I think it's a wonderful idea," said Mrs. Bradford.

Ben's eyes widened and he turned to protest.

"*Particularly*"—Mrs. Bradford halted him with a gesture—"if we can find out what he's been up to the past year."

A girl from the sports desk raised her hand. "His parents sent him to one of those survival schools in Canada. Tough Love or something."

"No, they didn't." Another girl rolled her eyes. "He was being homeschooled."

I was about to inform them of what Marcus had told me, but Ben interrupted.

"Come on, guys. Let's wait for Delilah's article." He turned back to the board, smirking, and added, "Besides, everyone knows he's been making license plates in juvie. The guy's too dumb to do anything else."

The other kids laughed at Ben's comment, but for some reason, I wasn't amused. Maybe it was because Ben was getting so much pleasure out of making Marcus look stupid when he wasn't around to defend himself.

At that moment, Ben looked over and smiled the same smile he'd given me when I'd rescued him from Marcus the year before. Even though he'd grown so much since then, I realized he still felt like a victim, and this was his way of fighting back. So, I smiled to let him know I was still on his side.

"Ava." Ben finished writing my new assignments—"changes to your story?"

She shook her head as she opened her binder. "In fact, I already have a completed proof." She made a big show of waving the article in my direction before laying it in front of Ben's chair. I knew she wanted a reaction from me, and I was more than happy to oblige.

Clearing my throat, I said, "I was wondering . . . is the school board okay with this?"

Ava responded in a voice that sounded flat as a tuba. "You *must* be joking."

"Well"—I looked innocently at her—"I'd hate for students to read your article and think shoplifting is a great way to get attention."

"I . . . didn't think about that," said Ben, frowning.

"Luckily, I did." I handed him the spiral page. "I thought it might upset some parents, so I called the school board. Six of the seven members don't want Ava telling their kids about the thrills of shoplifting."

"But . . . but that is *not* what I am doing!" Ava directed her protest at Ben, but her eyes flashed daggers at me.

Ben scanned the paper and passed it to Mrs. Bradford with a questioning look. "Do you think this will be okay?"

Mrs. Bradford pursed her lips. "Delilah, you said six of the seven members disapproved. What about the seventh?"

"Actually," I said, "he disapproved too, but—"

There was a knock on the door, and every spine of every

student instantly straightened as the headmaster of Brighton Junior Academy entered the room.

"The seventh member wanted to tell you in person," I finished.

I felt sorry for Mrs. Bradford, who blushed and tugged on her shirt to smooth it, and for Ben, who looked as if he wanted to climb inside the cap of the marker dangling from his hand.

When I saw the expression on Ava's face, however, I had to work hard to transform my victorious smile into an apologetic one. "Sorry, Ava."

"Good afternoon, everyone," said the headmaster, smiling. "We need to have a little chat."

Chapter Ten

That was wicked," Jenner whispered in my ear as we walked out of the journalism room. "I think I actually saw smoke coming out of Ava's ears."

I blew on my fingernails and shined them on my shirt. "All in a day's work."

"I just feel bad for Ben and Mrs. Bradford. They must be totally embarrassed."

I shook my head. "I told the headmaster *they* were the ones who wanted to make sure the article was okay."

"Nice!" Jenner slapped me five.

Ben emerged from the class and threw an arm around my neck, giving me a squeeze. "Thank you for the save. I can't imagine the trouble we would've been in."

I wished he could have stayed that close forever . . . or at least until college, but he pulled back when Ava strolled over.

"It was nothing." I looked at Ava, summoning up my best expression of concern. "But what are you going to do for a debut article now? I mean, didn't you put all your hopes and dreams on that idea?"

"How sweet of you to worry." Five sharp fingernails dug into my shoulder as Ava attempted to pulverize my collarbone in her grip.

I winced and wormed out from under her clutches. "Just keeping you in my thoughts," I said. "You know, the way you did for me this morning."

"And I will continue to think of you." Ava smiled, but her upper lip curled back to reveal her canines. "As long as we share the same interests."

Ava fixed her eyes on mine, and I returned the stare with a slight nod.

Ben studied our exchange curiously as Jenner crunched on her candy watch.

"Is something weird going on?" Ben whispered to her.

Jenner licked some of the sugar off her lips. "It's better if you don't know."

"Well"—Ben cut through the tension between Ava and me—"good luck with the Swirlie Bandit interview, Delilah." He fixed me with a serious expression. "You don't have to do this. The guy's a *stinking loser.*"

"She'll be fine." Ava positioned herself between Ben and me. "Let's go find something you can wear to the social. I am sure Delilah needs to shop for her date as well." She smirked, and I knew she imagined me *literally* shopping for a date.

She was in for a surprise . . . but then, so was Ben.

He waved as Ava dragged him down the hall by one hand, and it was all I could do not to yank on the other and pull him back to safety.

"See you guys later!" I yelled. He'd never catch the apology buried in it, but I couldn't very well blurt, "And stay away from toilets at the party!"

"You know Ava's going to get back at you," said Jenner. "I've seen enough horror movies to spot the vengeful look in someone's eye."

"I know, but I have the weekend to think about it. It's not like she'll try anything tomorrow night." I walked to my locker and found a piece of ripped-out notebook paper stuffed in the slats.

"The Little Debbies are getting cheap with their stationery," commented Jenner.

"It's from Marcus." I unfolded the paper and sighed. "He wants to make sure nobody thinks we're 'together,' so now he's going to meet me at the country club. Nice."

I had no idea why I'd ever felt bad for him.

Jenner squeezed my shoulder. "Remember, it's only one evening of torture, and you'll have a great article from it."

"Unless I have to spend the whole time keeping him and Ben from pummeling each other," I said, sniffing the air. "And Paige, I can smell you from here. What do you want?"

Paige strolled around the corner, filing her nails. "Oh, were the two of you having a private conversation? I didn't hear *any* of it." She pointed the file at me. "But *nice* that there are two guys willing to fight over you! Have you been wearing the new blush?"

"It's not that kind of fighting," I told her. "And again, I ask, what do you want?"

She drew herself up a little taller and transitioned to Presidential Paige. "Two things. First, how are you coming on your pledge task?"

"Aaaand I'm out." Jenner smiled apologetically. "Beach on Sunday?"

"I'll give you every grisly detail about the social," I assured her.

Exasperated, Paige sighed loudly to remind me that I was sharing airspace with her.

"Later." Jenner winked at me and scurried away.

I turned to Paige, feigning confusion. "Paige, when did you get here?"

"Ha-ha. Progress report. Now."

"The pledge task is going fine," I said. "I think something strange—something *big*—happened at Katie's old school. I'm going to visit next Monday and ask questions—maybe see if I can bump into Katie's old friends."

Paige allowed the corners of her mouth to slip into a smile. "Clever, but the teachers here are going to notice you're missing."

"I have a free period after lunch, and Jenner said she'd cover for me if I was late to class after that."

"And how do you plan to get across town without a car?"

I shrugged. "Same as I always do. I'll take the bus."

"Um . . . ew." Paige shuddered and winced. "You actually take . . . the bus?"

"Ever since my chauffeur quit, I don't have a choice."

"Funny." She narrowed her eyes at me. "Your plan is good. But I need more. I need proof that you're onto something."

"You want proof?" Making sure the coast was clear, I walked to a locker across from mine and pulled out a piece of paper I'd folded into my pocket. "It's amazing what you can find on the Internet, you know?"

Paige took the paper and read the title. "Cracking combination locks." She gasped and thrust the page back at me. "You're breaking and entering . . . and I'm an accomplice!"

"It's not breaking and entering unless Katie lives in here." I rapped on the metallic door, then pressed my ear to it and looked at the paper. "Besides, I'm not taking anything. I'm just browsing."

Paige cracked her gum, each snap emphasizing her disbelief. "Does Jennifer know you do this?"

"Her name's Jenner," I said, "and if she knew all the things I do for investigative reporting, we probably wouldn't be best friends." I turned the locker dial and listened for a click. "She has a problem with things that are slightly illegal."

"So do I! Especially when 'slightly illegal' sends you to the same jail as 'regular illegal.'" Paige smoothed her hair. "And I'm too pretty to wear orange."

I rolled my eyes. "We aren't going to jail. The worst that would happen is we'd get detention, but *I'd* take all the heat for it, anyway, so don't worry about it." The locker finally rewarded me with a click, and I looked up at the dial. "Remember the number forty-two."

"Forty-two, forty-two, forty-two." She paced back and forth. "The answer to life, the universe, and everything."

"Huh?" I spun the dial again and listened for a second click.

She waved me away. "My dad has it on one of his geeky T-shirts. Forty-two, forty-two, forty-two."

Paige's words shattered my concentration. "Your dad wears T-shirts *and* he's a geek?" I'd assumed he spent his time on a yacht sipping champagne, not playing video games. "How did *you* turn out so different?"

She glared at me. "What's that supposed to mean? I'm smart. I got a perfect score on the *Seventeen* personality test."

I rolled my eyes. "I mean geekdom is almost as genetic as freckles. I'm just surprised your dad doesn't rub off on you."

Paige shrugged. "He probably doesn't have enough *time* to rub off. I only get to see him once a month."

"Oh." That hadn't been the answer I expected. "Sorry."

"It's no big deal." She smirked, as if an apology were *so* out of fashion. "Can you imagine all the lame things he'd make me do if he were around? He'd probably take me to dorky movies and have me help him shop for better clothes." She laughed, but it sounded halfhearted and fake.

"Yeah." I forced a laugh too and got back to work, searching for the next number in the combination and the end to the awkwardness.

Paige leaned against the locker next to Katie's. "He's not in prison." The snotty tone had returned to her voice. "I know that's what you're thinking."

I shook my head. "Prisoners can have visitors every week,

so I never thought that. Remember the number fifteen." It wasn't the next number in the combination, but I could tell she needed a distraction.

Paige started chanting. "Forty-two, fifteen. Forty-two, fifteen. Forty-two . . . fine!" She stopped and turned to me, sighing deeply. "If you're going to make *such* a big deal of it, I'll tell you."

For once, I actually wasn't curious for dirt on someone's private life. "Um . . . okay."

"My dad left us, and my mom had a better lawyer, so she got full custody. She promised nothing would change, but she's so controlling." Her nostrils flared with emotion. "The only time I get to see him is when I sneak out during her monthly garden club meeting."

I'd found the last number to Katie's combination, but I didn't open the locker. I wasn't sure if it was worse to lose someone entirely, like I had, or to lose someone just enough to make it painful to see them again.

"Why don't you ask your mom to let you visit him?"

She rolled her eyes and snapped her gum. "Didn't you hear? I have absolutely *no* power over her."

This from the girl who controlled one of the most influential groups of students at Brighton. Or maybe that was *why* she controlled them . . . because the rest of her life wasn't up to her.

112

Paige frowned and pointed at the locker. "Have you figured this out or do we need to call a locksmith?"

"Oh. Right." I jerked on the lever and pulled the door open.

Katie's locker was surprisingly neat. The space had been sectioned off with colorful plastic shelves so that her textbooks rested on the bottom and her binders and personal effects lay across the middle. The top shelf, however, was a mystery.

"*What* is that?" Paige prodded at a red metallic ball, the only thing occupying the space. It was the size and shape of a grapefruit and had a nozzle mounted on top.

"Hair spray?" I suggested.

Paige shook her head. "Katie's hair doesn't look crunchy enough."

"Perfume?"

"In a container like that?" She sniffed at me. "It's not like you'd know, anyway."

I ignored her and chewed on my lip. "This might sound weird, but it kind of looks like a fire extinguisher. I'll search for it on the Internet when I get a chance."

I took my cell phone out and snapped a picture of the container, then moved on to the middle shelf, leafing through the contents. "Her date book! What—" I looked back at Paige just as she raised a glass bottle and squirted me with the contents, most of which found their way into my open mouth. "Ack!" I sputtered and gagged as the heady smell of perfume overwhelmed me. "You Chanel-ed me!"

"You weren't supposed to turn around," said Paige, "and I would *never* waste Chanel. This is Pink Sugar. I use it on my gym sneakers."

"I'm not allowed to wear perfume . . . or drink it!" I smacked my tongue against the roof of my mouth, making a face.

"Just tell your stepdad someone accidentally got you with it." She took the date book from me and flipped to October. "Ha! She doesn't have the Woodcliff Pumpkin Romp in here *or* any Halloween parties planned. But . . . she does have *this* whole week marked off."

Paige pointed at the first week of the month and frowned. Katie had drawn a line across the entire week, with the letters NFP written above it. "NFP . . . and on that Friday night there's a banquet." Paige gasped. "NF. Do you know what that is?"

"Some sort of awareness group." I wiped my face with the bottom of my shirt.

"No. Nouveau Fashion!" When I didn't cheer and wave pom-poms, Paige gave me a pained look. "They're one of the top designers on your fashion card. When was the last time you looked at it?"

"When I used it to scrape gum off my shoe. Listen, Katie said NFP was an awareness thing."

"An awareness of *fashion*, maybe." She tapped her finger-nails on her chin. "It must be their premiere week."

"Neat." I started fiddling around in Katie's locker again.

"Although why *she* got invited to the banquet and I didn't . . . Delilah, now you really have to take her down. She's stealing the exclusive invitations *I* should be getting."

"The *nerve* of that girl." I studied the inside of Katie's locker door. She *definitely* had an obsession with sea turtles. There were pictures of sea turtles swimming, pictures of her petting sea turtles, pictures of her in sea turtle T-shirts . . .

"Paige!"

"Hmm?" She continued to read the date book until I snatched it from her. "Hey!"

"When I talked to Katie on the beach, she said she *never* wore T-shirts, but look!" I stabbed the locker door so hard, it swung back into the one behind it.

"She's wearing T-shirts." Paige looked at the pictures, then at me. "You think that's her big secret? That she bares her elbows in private?"

I squeezed my fists into frustrated balls. "No! But why would she lie about that? And what's with this thing?" I grabbed the red metal globe. "There's something tying it all together, but . . ." I sighed. "I have to talk to her friends."

"Monday," Paige agreed. "But before then you have the Debutante social . . . which brings me to my second question." She closed Katie's locker door and spun me to face her. "What are you wearing tomorrow night?"

"Nothing," I mumbled, jotting myself a note about Katie's old schoolmates. "I don't own a single thing appropriate for a social. My options are a flower girl dress from when I was eight or a bath towel with sequins stapled to it. Take your pick."

For a moment, I was afraid she might take the bath towel option, just to punish me for making her life difficult, but she smiled and reached into her designer book bag.

"I had a feeling you might say that, so I brought you this." She withdrew a green bundle and let one end tumble from her fingers until it unfurled into a dress.

"Wow." I held up the dress to study it. "I didn't think rich people did the whole hand-me-down thing."

"Please." Paige laughed. "I got this for Christmas but never wore it, so I put it aside to give to the less fortunate." She gestured grandly at me. "And here you are!"

"Thanks." I was starting to miss the emotionally fragile Paige already.

"Anyway, green makes me look on the verge of ill, and even though you *never* dress to show your figure, I thought we might be about the same size."

The fabric was simple cotton, but the hem and waist were accented with silver beads. I had to admit it wasn't that bad . . . until I saw the neckline. Instead of a zippered collar, it was two lengths of ribbon tied together.

I was going to be a reporter in a halter top.

Paige watched me the entire time, and when I didn't squeal with girlish glee, she grunted in frustration. "You're not oohing and aahing!"

"I can't wear something so revealing. My stepdad would kill me."

"Which is why you hide it under this." She pulled a silver scarf out of the bag with a flourish and draped it around the dress. "*Now* what do you think?"

It was better than a towel and might actually get an admiring glance from Ben, but I was baffled that Paige had put so much effort into making sure I looked good. I wanted to ask, but I just took the dress.

"Thanks. I'll find a way to pay you for this."

"Just come up with a better clique story than Ava does," said Paige, "and *don't* embarrass me tomorrow night."

Chapter Eleven

W ho is this guy again?" Major stopped the car in front of the Brighton Country Club and reached into his coat pocket.

"Major"—I buried my face in my hands—"tell me you *didn't* bring a miniature version of the banned boy book."

"Of course not. . . . The print would be too small. These are just the names of the most serious offenders." He withdrew an index card and held it up.

Marcus was at the very top of the list.

"Gordon Elliott," I said automatically. "I'm meeting a guy named Gordon Elliott. I doubt he's on there."

I *knew* he wasn't. Earlier I'd peeked at Major's book and chosen the most harmless-looking guy in green marker, a seventh grader who snorkeled at the school pool during lunch hour.

Major scanned the index card and nodded. "All right, then. But I want you to take this to be safe." He handed me a tiny spray canister.

"Uh . . . no. I'm not going to Mace any of my class-mates."

"This is cinnamon extract. It stings just as much when sprayed in the eyes, but the effects don't last as long." He forced it into my palm. "Also, the smell triggers memory functions, so your date will *remember* not to attack you in the future."

"He's not my date." I dropped the cinnamon spray into the silver purse left over from my flower girl days. "I'm just showing up with him because I can't go alone."

I looked out the car window and almost jumped when I saw Marcus standing by the entrance to the country club. I ducked my head so my hair hung over my face, but I quickly realized it was a terrible disguise since I was the only redhead pledging the Little Debbies. Still, I peeked at him through my dangling strands.

Marcus had actually skipped his usual sports ensemble and worn a button-up shirt *and* tucked it into his jeans. If he'd bothered to brush his hair, which stood up in odd, spiky tufts, he could have passed for someone fairly gorgeous.

"I should get going," I told Major. "Gordon's probably waiting inside."

Major peered around me. "He should have waited for you out here, like that young gentleman is doing for *his* date." He pointed at Marcus, who chose that moment to glance in my direction. "You know, he looks vaguely familiar."

Up until that point, I'd never believed in mental telepathy, but I focused all my concentration on melding my mind with his.

Don't come over here, I thought. *Do something gross so Major stops staring.*

Marcus missed the second half of my message, but he seemed to catch the first bit and turned away, gazing across the parking lot.

"Gotta go," I blurted at Major, fumbling for the door handle. "Pick me up at nine. Thanks!"

I closed the car door behind me, and then Major pulled a parental maneuver straight from the *How to Embarrass Your Teen* manual. He rolled down the passenger-side window and called across the car, "He won't be afraid to make a move, so don't be afraid to spray him!"

Luckily, nobody was close enough to hear this gem of wisdom but me. "Okay. Bye!" I smiled and waved until he pulled away from the curb. As soon as the car was out of sight, Marcus strolled over, smirking.

"Spray him, huh? Did you pack a garden hose in there?" He nudged my purse. "And don't worry. This is as close as I *ever* plan to get to you."

Even though Marcus was a known jerk, I couldn't help feeling a little offended. I'd checked my reflection just before leaving the house and thought I looked pretty. *And* I'd been nice enough to notice his improved appearance—I just hadn't mentioned it out loud.

I gave him my biggest, fakest smile. "You *really* know how to make a girl feel special. Thank you."

Marcus looked a trifle less smug. "I told you this wasn't a date. . . . And it's not like I said you looked bad or anything."

"Let's just get this over . . ." I jerked the door open and stepped into the foyer but didn't move any farther. "Yikes."

My parents had never been country club people, so my knowledge of that world was limited to what I saw on television. Usually everything was white wicker and windows, with sunlight bathing young tennis couples as they laughed and sipped iced tea, served by a cheerful waiter in a starched uniform.

The Brighton Country Club was not like that.

Everything was cold and dark. The walls were paneled in ebony wood, and the carpet was a deep wine color that spilled into two wings branching off the main room. Sconces lit the way, each just bright enough to reveal the next one down the hall. Massive leather chairs had replaced (or possibly eaten) the wicker furniture, along with the laughing tennis couple. The only person in sight was a thousand-year-old woman who was watching us with a critical eye and pointing down one of the hallways.

"Jenner would love it here," I said. "It's like . . ."

"A funeral home?" Marcus ran his fingers along the wood paneling. "Or a haunted house?"

I couldn't help smiling. "A little of both. You ready?"

Marcus tugged at his collar and cleared his throat. "Listen. Earlier, I really didn't say you looked bad."

"Yeah, but . . ." I wanted to argue that he hadn't said I looked *good*, either, but I realized this was the closest he would ever come to paying me a compliment. "Thanks." I returned to all business before things could get awkward. "*Now* are you ready?"

He let out a deep breath. "Not really, but I don't think she plans to leave until we do." He nodded to the old woman, still standing with her arm outstretched. "Come on."

Even though the hallway was wide enough for us to

walk several feet apart, we drifted closer together with each step. It was strangely comforting to be with someone who felt just as awkward, and from the way Marcus's arm kept bumping mine, I knew he was thinking the same thing. As we passed the woman, he whispered, "Your spirit is free, old one. You've done your duty."

I laughed but stopped short when a guy and a Little Debbie hurried past us, and I was almost blinded by her crystal-covered tiara.

She was wearing a *tiara*. I didn't even own a headband. And her heels were high enough to cause serious head trauma if she were to stumble.

"Man, I knew I should have worn my crown jewels," I said.

Marcus didn't seem to catch my joke. "*I* should have worn a tie," he mumbled. "Or different shoes."

For someone who'd spent sixth grade shoving people's heads into toilets, he seemed awfully concerned about opinions now. Maybe he *had* changed since his Swirlie Bandit days.

"You look fine," I told him. "*That* kid's the overdressed one. I mean, what twelve-year-old wears cuff links?"

He nodded. "I was just hoping to make a good impression, like you said at the beach."

"Oh. Right. The beach." I pressed my lips together

before a guilty confession could slip out. He'd actually taken me seriously and wanted to improve his social standing, but I'd brought him for my own amusement. Now I felt bad. I needed to hate him. I needed to interview him and hear him say he couldn't wait to dunk more kids.

But first I needed to check on Ben and Ava.

They weren't hanging around with the few couples outside the Crystal Ballroom, but I did see the girl from the Little Debbies gift bag table. She was sitting at yet *another* table outside the doorway, and this time she was in charge of a stack of purple picture frames and stick-on name tags. I wandered over to her, wondering how much money she'd be after this time.

"Name?" Table Girl addressed my midsection.

"I can write my own name tag," I said, grabbing a Sharpie.

Table Girl slammed her hand on top of mine, as if I'd been trying to pocket her marker and run away. "Your name tag is over *here.*" She pointed to the stack of picture frames, and I indicated the one with my name on it.

When she gave it to me, my hand dropped a little from the weight. I turned the frame over and saw someone had glued a giant safety pin to the back.

"Do I really have to wear this?"

She answered me with a sour look, so I pinned the picture

frame to my purse. "It clashes with my dress," I explained.

"Whatever." She uncapped the Sharpie and turned to Marcus. "Name?"

"Marcus."

Instead of writing, she stared at him.

"Marcus," he repeated louder.

"I know," she said. "But unless you're Fergie, you should have a last name too."

"Taylor. I'm Marcus Taylor."

"The Swirlie Bandit!?" Table Girl's cry demonstrated a lung power I wouldn't have thought possible of a Little Debbie. Like choreographed dancers, the other couples all whirled and glanced at us, faces frozen in varying stages of alarm.

Marcus turned red, the spikes in his hair needing no gel to help them stand on end. "I . . . uh . . . don't really go by that. I haven't dunked anyone since I left school."

Table Girl's eyes widened and she sucked in her breath. "You dropped out?"

"No! I mean, since the first time I left to go to a different school."

"Ohhh." She nodded and winked. "A 'school' behind a wall of razor wire?"

"Okay, we're gonna go now." I was starting to get the same irritated feeling from Friday morning, when Ben had been insulting Marcus for no reason. This time Marcus could defend himself, so it shouldn't have bothered me—but it did.

I grabbed his arm and as we walked away, I could hear Table Girl tell everyone, "They really should screen pledges better to find out who they're dating."

Marcus didn't argue or even laugh at the *D* word. He seemed to be interested in drawing as little attention to himself as possible, and when we walked into the Crystal Ballroom, he hurried off to the left, away from the dance floor and the tables surrounding it.

I dug my heels into the carpet and tugged him to a halt. "Okay, if this is your idea of making a good impression, it's not working."

"It's never going to work," he said. "I've changed my mind. You don't have to interview me."

"Well, I already told everyone I would, so I kinda do." I glanced around for the darkest, most secluded table I could find. "We can go over there. By that window." I steered him toward it just as Paige hurried over.

"*What* are you doing?"

"Being antisocial at the social," I said.

"I *mean* with him." She pointed at Marcus as if he were twenty feet away, not close enough for her to poke in the shoulder. "You brought the Swirlie Bandit?"

Marcus cleared his throat. "Actually, I don't—"

Paige blocked him with a hand to the face. "I *told* you not to embarrass me, Delilah!"

I thought I'd enjoy seeing her freak out, but even the fact that her face matched the pink in her dress didn't amuse me. "It's not a big deal," I said. "He's changed, and nobody at the social is in danger of a dunk and flush. But if you'd rather we leave . . ." I grabbed Marcus's arm and made like I was headed for the door.

"Wait . . ." Paige tugged on the halter straps tied around my neck. "You have to at least stay for another half hour, when everyone gives their progress reports." She eyed Marcus suspiciously and leaned close to me. "Just keep him under control and out of the way."

I nodded. "Do you want me to chain him to the wall or just hit him with my shoe whenever he acts up?"

Paige crossed her arms and exhaled out of her nostrils. "Whatever . . . it . . . takes." She stormed off to yell at someone for double-dipping chips in a bowl of guacamole.

I rolled my eyes at Marcus. "Let's try this again." I headed for the window, but he didn't follow. "Marcus?"

"I'm gonna go." He nodded toward the door. "This was a really bad idea."

It *was* a bad idea . . . even worse than my Renee Mercer story. But I needed the interview, and I couldn't be dateless when Ava waltzed in with Ben. "If you leave," I said, "everyone's going to think it's because they're onto you and that you haven't really changed. You have to *show* them that you're not a threat . . . and you can't do that if you're not here."

He sighed and dropped his shoulders. "I know."

"*And* you can also show them by talking about what *really* happened." I started walking toward the window again, and this time he followed me. I sat at the table and pulled a mini cassette recorder from my bag. "Why did you do it?"

When I flipped the recorder on, Marcus didn't answer right away.

"The first time I did it . . ." He spoke slowly, thinking about each word. "The first time it was to prove a point."

"That you *could* fit someone's head in a toilet?"

Marcus smirked. "There was this kid . . . this eighth grader who kept calling me a wimp. So, I dunked him."

I frowned. "An eighth grader? I thought your first victim was someone from our class."

Marcus shook his head, then realized my tape recorder wouldn't catch that. "No, but the guy wasn't going to admit that he'd been flushed by a sixth grader, so nobody ever found out about it."

"But you had your revenge," I pointed out. "Why didn't it stop there?"

Marcus looked at me with a twinkle in his eyes. "Because it was fun. It was power. And even if kids didn't know who did it, for a moment, I wasn't . . ." He faltered, and the spark of happiness fizzled out.

"You weren't what?" I prompted.

He shifted in his chair and watched the other students.

"Marcus, you weren't what?" I repeated.

"Do you know all these people?" He pointed to a couple admiring an ice sculpture shaped like a giant high heel.

"A-a little," I stuttered in my confusion. "The girl's in the drama department, and her date's some guy who wins the talent show every year."

Marcus nodded. "Everyone knows them."

Now I understood what he was getting at. "But they didn't know you. You were—"

"Invisible." He folded his hands on the table and studied the thumbs.

We sat quietly while the cassette player continued to record our silence. I'd never been invisible; writing for the paper made sure of that. But if I hadn't gotten involved in any school activities . . . if I'd been a loner, I wondered what I might have done to feel like I mattered.

"Well," I finally said, "you definitely have everyone's attention now."

Marcus glanced up at me. "Yeah, I guess I do." One corner

of his mouth turned up. "Of course, this wasn't exactly what I had in mind."

I laughed. "Well, what did you have in mind? Tell me everything you'd like people to know about the Swir—" I stopped myself. "About Marcus Taylor."

Chapter Twelve

Interviewing Marcus turned out to be less painful than I'd expected. The entire time we talked, he didn't remind me once that I'd ruined his life, and, as it turned out, he *had* been doing a lot since he'd left Brighton. He'd been the Snappin' Sea Turtle mascot at Sheldon Academy, played striker in the local soccer league (and helped them win the district championship), *and* been a movie extra the previous summer.

"No way." I grinned. "You . . . an actor?"

"An *extra*," he pointed out. "I pretty much walked through the scene and that was it, but I got to meet Fritz Fulton." He pulled out his cell phone and showed me a picture of him with possibly the hottest teen actor of all time.

"That is so cool. I got my picture taken with a celebrity this summer too." I handed over my cell phone and Marcus groaned.

"Smokey the Bear?"

I laughed. "When we went camping, my stepfather made us sit through a fire safety seminar before we could strike a single match."

Marcus clicked through my pictures. "That explains this one of a fire extinguisher . . . I guess." He smiled at me. "Were you afraid you wouldn't remember what it looked like?"

He flipped the phone around so I could see the image. It was the red globe from Katie's locker.

"So, it *is* a fire extinguisher!" I grabbed the cell phone from him.

"Yeah. There's the handle to fire off the foam." He pointed at the nozzle. "You really didn't pay attention during that seminar, did you?"

"Who keeps something like this in their locker?" I jumped up from my seat, scanning the room for Paige, and saw her at a chocolate fountain, dipping strawberries . . . with Ava and Ben.

"Crap!" I sat down just as quickly without considering the attention my jack-in-the-box antics would draw. Ben glanced over, squinting into the darkness, and waved. Luckily, Marcus's back was turned. I waved and got up again, intending to hurry over to Ben before he could see Marcus.

"I'll be back. Just sit here and don't turn around."

Knowing his disregard for rules, I should have predicted what would happen next.

Marcus stood up . . . and turned around. "Who were you waving at?"

I stepped in front of him. "Ben Hines, the guy you were attacking when I caught you last year."

"Really?" He peered around me. "He looks a lot different."

I glanced over my shoulder and saw Ben doing the same thing, trying to figure out who my date was.

"He's grown," I said. "And he *really* doesn't like you."

A rational person would have said "Yikes" and sat back down, but Marcus said, "I'll go talk to him"—and headed straight for Ben.

"Oh, this won't end well." I followed on his heels.

The closer Marcus got to Ben, the darker Ben's expression became, until there was practically a storm brewing in his eyes. Ava fixed me with a similar glare.

"Hey . . . Ben," said Marcus. "I was wondering if we could talk."

"What are *you* doing here?" Ben was taking full advantage of his new, deep voice to practically growl at Marcus. "Shouldn't you be waiting by the punch bowl to shove people into it?"

"He's with me." I said. "And he's not here to cause trouble."

Ben recoiled as if I'd slapped him. "You're dating this loser?"

"How shocking," said Ava in a sarcastic tone that indicated it wasn't.

"We're not dating," I said. "I'm interviewing him for my article."

"And I just came over to apologize," said Marcus.

Ben's anger faded a little. "You did?"

"You did?" I was just as surprised.

Ben reached past Ava and grabbed my hand. My fingers instantly tingled, and I prayed nobody could see the goose bumps on my arms. "Come talk to me for a second." He led me out of the room and over to the leather couches in the foyer.

"Please tell me you're not dating that guy," he said.

"I already told you no." I did my best to act offended, but I was secretly pleased.

Ben was jealous of me and Marcus.

"Good," he said. "Because he isn't the guy you should be with."

My heart threatened to pry my jaws apart and leap onto the floor. "Who . . . who *should* I be with?"

Ben scooted closer and grabbed both my hands. "Someone who has a plan for his future and is smart and funny and knows how to treat you right."

"I completely agree," I said, bowing my head modestly. "But who could *that* be?"

"Delilah, I don't know why I didn't tell you this sooner, but . . ." He leaned toward me, speaking in a whisper. I could smell his cologne and the chocolate on his breath. His mouth was close enough to kiss.

So I did.

I rose off my seat, grabbed his face, and pressed my lips against his chocolaty, strawberry ones. I knew I wasn't supposed to watch, but I wanted to have a visual memory of every moment of my first kiss. I gazed up into Ben's eyes, but instead of seeing the same bliss that I felt, I saw only confusion. My stomach tightened as he placed his hands on my shoulders and pushed me back.

He didn't like me.

I'd attacked him with my lips and let him know how I really felt—and he didn't like me.

"What are you doing?" he asked. "I'm with Ava."

"Well, I . . . I thought . . ." I bit my lower lip to keep it from trembling, and brushed my hair back several times, my cheeks aching with suppressed emotion. "You said that . . . that I should be with . . . I thought you meant—" The last word caught in my throat, drowned in the beginnings of a sob. I could feel the tears building behind my eyes, and my nose started to run.

I jumped off the couch and sprinted down the hall opposite the Crystal Ballroom, looking for a door to hide behind . . . preferably one that led to some alternate universe where I hadn't kissed Ben. I spotted a ladies' room and ducked inside, collapsing onto a chaise lounge in the waiting area, where I promptly burst into tears.

I'd never been so wrong or so embarrassed about something in my entire life. Kissing Ben had been such an impulsive and *stupid* thing to do, especially since he *already had a girlfriend* and was my editor on the newspaper. My levelheadedness had always been one of my best traits, but ever since I'd seen "the new Ben," that had fallen by the wayside. I should have known better. I wasn't the kind of girl who won at romance. I was going to be the thirty-year-old lady having dinner conversations with her cats.

"Delilah?"

I smelled Chanel and then felt Paige sit beside me, her arm wrapped around my shoulder. "What happened? I know it can't be the dress, because that looks fabulous."

Despite myself, I blubbered a laugh and wiped at my eyes.

"Oh, sweetie, don't do that. You're not wearing waterproof mascara." Paige grabbed a tissue and dabbed at the black lines trailing down my cheeks. "Was this about a guy?"

I nodded and sniffled. "How did you guess?"

"Because I've never seen *anything* get you down before." She crumpled up the tissue and smiled. "And because it's *always* about a guy."

While she reapplied my makeup, I calmed down and told her what had happened. "I guess I'm a fool," I ended the story.

She nodded and swiped blush across my cheek. "I'd have to agree with that."

"Hey!" I pulled back, frowning.

"Well, I *did* tell you he was lame." She grabbed my jaw and turned my head from side to side. "God, I wish I had your cheekbones."

"I wish I had an escape route." I walked to a hanging mirror to study my reflection. Paige had actually succeeded in making my face look like nothing had gone wrong. If only she could apply the same flawless coverage to my life. "He's going to be out there. I know it."

"Well, you can't spend the rest of your life hiding in here." She wrinkled her nose. "This is a public restroom, for crying out loud."

"You're right." I stood tall and threw my shoulders back.

"I have to act like I didn't run away, wailing like an infant."

Paige shook her head. "You actually ran in a fancy party dress? We have *got* to work on your poise. If you become a Debutante, that'll be your *next* task."

Her comment reminded me of how the mess with Ben had started in the first place. "Hey, I meant to tell you earlier—remember that thing in Katie's locker that looked like a time bomb? I was right. It's a fire extinguisher."

Paige mulled this over. "Hmmm . . . a girl with a clique named Hot Stuff has a fire extinguisher in her locker. That's very . . . what's the word? Iconic."

"Ironic," I corrected her. "But the big question is, why does she have one? Is she planning something that involves potential fire hazard?"

Paige's eyes widened. "Some big publicity event that'll make Hot Stuff even more popular?"

I gave her a strange look. "I think I'd be more concerned for the *safety* of the student body."

"Right. That, too. Now you *really* have to find out her deep, dark secret." She smiled. "And that gives us more dish for your progress report tonight." She checked her cell phone. "Which it's about time for. You ready to face the world?"

I took a deep breath and swallowed hard. "I'm ready to face anything."

As it turned out, I wasn't.

When I'd fled for the ladies' room earlier, the foyer had been empty except for the thousand-year-old woman and Ben. It had also been quiet. Now it was crowded with students who were yelling and standing in a semicircle around two figures engaged in a serious smackdown.

"Oh, no," I whispered.

Ben and Marcus had their upper bodies completely entwined, pushing at each other inside the half circle, while Ava stomped around them, shouting, "Stop this! You are acting like children!"

"Marcus, don't!" I added my voice to the chaos, regretting it seconds later.

Marcus glanced up at me, and while he was distracted, Ben seized the chance to kick a leg behind him and knock him to the ground.

"Stop!" I ran toward them, and Paige groaned.

"Poise, Delilah! Poise!"

I ignored her and reached into my purse for the cinnamon spray Major had forced on me. "Stop or I'll spray!" I threatened.

Ben and Marcus froze for half a second, looked at my tiny canister, and got to their feet to resume their country club brawl. I darted into the center of the semicircle and raised the cinnamon spray. As I held down the trigger, however,

Ava ran forward from the opposite side, waving her purse wildly in the air, as if she planned to knock both guys senseless.

They moved to avoid her *and* me, which placed Ava directly into the cinnamon spray firing range, and I shot her square in the eyes.

No threats or yelling could have broken up the fight, but Ava's shrieks of pain and rage quieted the entire room. She collapsed and flailed on the carpet, clutching at her face.

"Ava, I'm sorry!" I threw the spray aside and dropped to the floor beside her. "I'm so sorry. I didn't mean to hurt you."

"Liar!!" Ava pulled her hands down just long enough for me to see that the whites of her eyes were bright red and that tears were streaming down her face. "You kiss my boyfriend and attack me? You want to do *nothing* but hurt me, you—" She launched a slew of words at me in French and kicked in my direction. I dodged the pointed end of her shoe and reached for her arm.

"Come on, you have to rinse it off with water."

A hand gripped my arm firmly and tugged me back. "I'll take care of her," said Paige. "You guys should go." Her gaze included Ben and Marcus.

"I'm really sorry," I told her, and I meant it. My plan to bring Marcus hadn't included soap opera drama.

"Don't be. You didn't start this fight." Paige helped Ava

to her feet. "I mean, technically you did, because it was about you, but you didn't *physically* start the fight." She paused. "Unless you count kissing Ben as physical." She waved me away. "Just go before I change my mind."

I walked out the front entrance, not giving either Ben or Marcus a single look, and sat on the sidewalk to call Major.

"Your cinnamon spray really works," I told him. "Would you come get me?"

He freaked out for a moment until I told him I'd used it on Ava, not on my imaginary date.

"I'll be there in ten minutes," he said. "And we can talk about it if you want."

"Thanks, Major." I hung up and brought my knees to my chest, resting my chin on them.

Marcus walked up and sat down beside me. "You sure know how to show a guy a good time."

"Sorry," I said, staring into space. "You were right. The social *was* a bad idea."

He patted me on the back. "At least you got to kiss a guy. Not your date, but—"

I glared at him. "What's that supposed to mean? You and I weren't *on* a date, remember? I was interviewing you for a story."

"You didn't tell anyone besides Ava and Ben that. For all they knew, we were dating, and you wandered off to make out with someone else." He gave me a thumbs-up. "That makes me look *really* good."

"Oh . . . my . . . God!" I got to my feet and kicked him in the thigh. "You can't possibly be turning this into something about you."

Marcus got to his feet too. "You're right. I forgot everything is always about Delilah."

"It is not!" I could feel my stupid, stupid tears threatening to make their reappearance. "If I'd known you were going to get upset, I wouldn't have kissed him!"

I froze the moment the words left my mouth. Marcus froze too and just stared at me. "What do you mean?"

I had no idea what I'd meant. I had no idea why I'd said it. All I knew was that I really *wouldn't* have kissed Ben if Marcus had a problem with it.

At that moment, I realized something that made me want to run and hide in the ladies' room all over again.

I sort of liked Marcus.

And he was sort of waiting for me to answer.

"What I meant was . . . you were nice enough to . . . uh . . . do the interview," I ad-libbed. "And you're right. It was rude of me to just leave like that."

"Oh." Marcus nodded. "Okay."

I cleared my throat. "What . . . um . . . were you and Ben fighting about, anyway?"

"Well, after you wandered off, I decided to find out what was up. When I got to the lobby, you were running away, crying, so I asked Ben what had happened. He got all defensive, one thing led to another, and then he sucker punched me."

I frowned. "He what?"

"He hit me when I wasn't ready." Marcus bent and held back the hair above his right ear, revealing a large welt.

"Whoa. Does it hurt?" I pushed on it, and he winced. "Sorry. And sorry he hit you." Over the past few hours I'd become a pro at dishing out apologies.

"It's not a big deal." He grinned. "I guess Ben and I are even now."

I had to agree with him, but I started to wonder about my own situation. I had hurt and humiliated Ava. We definitely *weren't* even, and I knew she'd want to settle the score.

How she would do it was the question.

Chapter Thirteen

"Here. You need these more than I do." Jenner handed me a bag of jelly beans from her beach tote. It was Sunday morning, and I'd joined her at the surf shop to interview her for the paper and to fill her in on the disaster that was the Little Debbies' social.

"Thanks." I ripped the bag open and searched for the purple ones. "Any chance these are magic beans? With the power to erase people's memories?"

She gave me a sympathetic look. "You can always change schools. That's what Marcus did."

I shook my head and crunched through the sugary shell of a purple bean. "I can't let Ava have the newspaper. I mean, I feel bad for what happened, but if I give up, she wins."

"Then let her!" Jenner groaned. "You have to stop this obsession. It isn't healthy."

Even though Jenner was my best friend, sometimes it felt like she didn't know me at all. Competition was what I loved, and being the best was all I wanted.

"If I let Ava win," I said, "she becomes the lead reporter, which means I'm stuck writing articles about Halloween safety and which lunch lady bought a new hairnet. Those kinds of stories don't get Junior Global Journalist Awards."

"Yes, but you avoid the embarrassment of kissing guys who don't like you."

I narrowed my eyes. "How many more times do you honestly think I'll do that?"

"I don't know." She grinned. "I never thought you'd do it a first time."

I shoved her. "Let's just get started on your interview."

We spent the next half hour talking about her surfing and her views on gender stereotypes, and then we wandered down to the beach so she could show me her new maneuvers. The longer she practiced, the warmer the sun felt, and after a while I fled toward the boardwalk for shade.

To my surprise, Katie Glenn was already there, resting

against a large boulder and wearing a hooded sweater. When she saw me, she stiffened.

"Sorry," I said. "I didn't come to bug you. I didn't know anyone was even down here."

Her shoulders relaxed into a bored shrug. "I don't own the beach. You can go wherever you want." She twisted her lips into a leer. "Just don't try to steal my boyfriend."

Thankfully, it was too dark under the boardwalk for her to see me blush. "Oh . . . ha! So, you heard about that?" At least she wasn't making smooching sounds, like the kid down my street, or saying she'd accept payment in kisses, like the jerk at the hot dog stand.

"Who hasn't?"

I actually wondered the same thing. "Well, in case you cared—"

"I don't." Katie leaned back against the rock, wiping her forehead on her sweater sleeve.

"You're not going to get sunburned under here," I said. "I think it's safe to at least roll up your sleeves."

For some reason, this earned me a sour look from Katie. "I'm fine. Mind your own business."

Unfortunately, I couldn't. Even if I hadn't been pledging the Little Debbies, I still had an insane curiosity about this girl and her fire extinguisher and sweaters and obsession with sea turtles.

"Why *do* you like sea turtles so much?" I asked.

In my opinion, the question was harmless enough that Katie couldn't say the answer would destroy her reputation . . . unless her father was a sea turtle or something.

Luckily, she seemed to agree. "The sea turtle is the mascot for my old school. I guess I just think they're kind of cool."

"Oh," I said, but Katie's words triggered a strange tingling sensation in my brain.

When I'd interviewed her before, she'd said her previous school was Fowler, home of Panther Pride. There were no sea turtle fans at Fowler.

But there were at Sheldon Academy.

"Well, bye. I hope you see some." I hurried back to my towel, signaling Jenner, but she was too busy paddling out to another wave, so I pulled out my cell phone and called Paige.

"Yes, you're still eligible to pledge the Debutantes," she answered.

"Huh?" I'd been so focused on the whole embarrassment factor that the thought had never crossed my mind. "I mean, oh, right. Phew!" I wiped imaginary sweat off my brow, even though she couldn't see it.

"I know you probably stayed up all night worrying," said Paige, "which means you have hideous bags under your eyes. Cucumber slices can help with that. . . . And you can use the leftovers to make a really healthy salad."

Before she could babble on with a list of ingredients, I interrupted. "Actually, I wanted to tell you that I caught Katie in another lie. This time, it's about her old school."

Paige was silent for a moment. "This girl gets stranger and stranger. Her secret must be *stellar*!"

"Listen, I have to call someone else. Do you have the school directory?"

"Somewhere." I heard her rummaging around. "Who are you looking for?"

"Marcus Taylor."

Paige made a cooing sound into the phone. "You already miss your new boyfriend?"

My cheeks warmed. "He's not my boyfriend, but he *did* go to the same school as Katie last year."

Paige gasped. "Brilliant!" She recited the number and I wrote it on my spiral notepad. "Now, when you call him, don't act like you *want* to talk to him," she advised.

I frowned. "But I *do* want to talk to him."

"No, you *don't*. Act like you dialed his number by mistake."

She was rapidly slipping into the void of insanity. "But he knows I don't know his number," I said. "How could I accidentally call it by mistake?"

"Tell him you were dialing some other number and missed it by a digit. Let's see. What place has a phone number almost like his? Let me get my other phone book."

I flipped my phone shut while she was still talking and looked at Marcus's number. Even though I had a legitimate reason to call him, my palms were damp with sweat. After one deep breath I took the plunge and punched in his digits.

"Hello?" Marcus answered.

At that moment, my throat chose to fill with phlegm, so that I gurgled "Hey" in a voice that sounded like I'd been gargling Jell-O.

"Who is this?" I could hear mild annoyance in his voice and tried to think of a clever explanation. I must have been quiet longer than I thought, because Marcus hung up.

"Argh!" I snapped the phone shut, and a minute later, it rang back with Marcus's phone number. I cleared my throat and tried again. "Hey, Marcus."

"Hey, Delilah." This time he didn't sound grossed out. I might have been imagining it, but he even sounded kind of . . . pleased. "I *thought* it was you."

"Oh, you speak Phlegm?"

"My caller ID does." He laughed. "I was wondering how you were doing, but it sounds like you're back to your old self."

I dug my foot into the sand and blushed. "Is that a bad thing?"

"Sometimes," he said. "Not always."

I wanted to ask him what he meant by "not always," but I had something else to take care of first. "I was actually calling about Katie Glenn."

"Oookay. Why?"

"There's something strange about her, and I know you went to her old school, so I have a feeling you know what it is. I want you to tell me."

"Oh." Marcus quieted for a beat. "In that case, no. Next subject."

My jaw dropped, and I just sat there, stupefied.

"Hello?"

"Why . . . why won't you tell me?" I managed.

"Because."

I was getting *really* tired of everyone being so vague. "'Because' is not an answer. Why not, Marcus?"

"Because I know whatever I tell you, you'll use it against her, and I also know what it feels like to have someone call you out and make you feel stupid, *Delilah*."

Pleasant Marcus had apparently handed the phone over to Bitter Marcus. Still, he had made a good point, and I recovered nicely with a fail-proof argument of my own.

"So?"

Marcus seemed baffled by this. "So . . . I'm not going to help you hurt her."

I flopped back on my towel. "Why do you care what happens to Katie, anyway? Was she your girlfriend or something?"

The thought hadn't occurred to me before, but it made me sit up straight. "That's it, isn't it? She was your girlfriend. Your partner in some crime you *both* committed at Sheldon."

"No!" Marcus groaned. "I've never had a girlfriend, and I'm starting to think I don't really ever want one."

"But you're not saying the two of you *didn't* commit a crime."

"I didn't commit any crime!" he practically yelled.

My heart started beating faster, and I shifted on my towel with nervous energy. "You're still not saying *she* didn't commit a crime, Marcus. She did, didn't she? She committed a crime, and that's why she changed schools!"

Marcus made a few grunting noises and said, "Just call me back when you're done playing reporter." And he hung up.

But he never denied that Katie had committed a crime.

I grinned.

And he wanted me to call him back.

I grinned a little wider.

Jenner plopped down beside me. "Those jelly beans did the trick, huh?"

An hour later, Jenner and I were wandering through the archives section of the public library.

"Why are we looking at old newspapers and *not* searching the Internet?" asked Jenner.

"Because whatever Katie did was big, but it wasn't big enough to make front page news. If it wasn't big news, it won't pop up on the Internet, and the county daily doesn't archive on their website beyond the current season."

I opened one of the cabinets of microfilm and pulled out six canisters labeled "September–December" of the previous year. "Katie's crime had to have happened during her fall semester of sixth grade, because she transferred to Brighton this past spring, so if we look through the local news on each of these, we should find *something*."

I loaded the earliest-dated microfiche into the reader and advanced through the images until I reached the local news, giving each page a quick scan for mention of Sheldon Academy.

Jenner grabbed another reel and eyed it suspiciously. "How many newspapers are on each of these?"

"I think the librarian said twenty."

"Which means we have to go through"—she noted the number of canisters on the table—"a *hundred and twenty* papers?"

"Um . . ." I looked up at her and smiled. "I love you? You're pretty and smart and have nice hair?"

She sighed and sat at a microfiche reader beside me. "Save it for Paige."

We skimmed through newspaper pages for two hours, our necks starting to cramp and our eyes blurring from watching the words whiz by. Finally, when I was beginning to feel as if my body had frozen into a hunched shell, Jenner bumped my arm.

"Check this out."

I leaned over to her screen and smiled at what I saw:

INVESTIGATORS STILL BAFFLED BY SHELDON FIRE

"Bingo." I printed out the article and read it while Jenner went in search of a vending machine.

According to the article, the fire at Sheldon Academy had happened over the weekend of November 15 in the science lab. There were no signs of forced entry into the school and no indication as to what had caused the fire. The entire lab had been damaged *except* for a special tank containing a *juvenile green sea turtle* brought in by the local marine center for students to discuss that week. The tank had been found on the front lawn of the school with the turtle still safely housed inside.

I read the article several times until Jenner reappeared with a package of Skittles for both of us.

"So, does Katie have pyrokinetic powers like in *Fire-starter*? Should I start wearing flame-retardant clothes to school?"

I shook my head and filled her in on the article. "I know who, what, when, and where. But I don't know why."

"As in, why would she torch her school?"

"Exactly. And how did she never get caught?"

I advanced through the microfiche in search of a follow-up article but found only a brief snippet saying that the police had decided to rule the fire an unsolved case, most likely the result of a prank gone wrong. Two months later, after the buzz had died down, Katie had transferred to Brighton.

She named her clique Hot Stuff, I assumed, in honor of her brief career as an arsonist, but that didn't explain the fire extinguisher in her locker or her motives. But I knew the answers to these questions would be found at her old school.

I fished my cell phone out of my bag and dialed Marcus. Jenner didn't know that I'd sort of started liking him, so I did my best to act professional.

"Delilah?" He made no effort to hide his surprise. "I didn't think you'd ever call back." His voice lowered a bit. "It's cool that you did, though."

I blushed and winced, already feeling guilty for what I was about to say. "I was . . . actually calling because I need a favor."

His simple reply spoke volumes of disappointment. "Oh."

"But later I can—"

"Don't worry about it. What did you want?" His tone changed to the Marcus I'd run into last week, the one who couldn't have cared less if Renee Mercer pummeled me into the ground. I tried not to seem flustered.

"I . . . uh . . . I . . . need to borrow part of your uniform from Sheldon. The sweater . . . if you still have it. Please."

"Okay. Is that it? I have to go."

My shoulders sagged and I bit my lip. He wasn't even remotely curious why I wanted the sweater. He just wanted to stop talking to me. "Yeah. Thanks." I snapped the phone shut and Jenner prodded my shoulder.

"What, may I ask, do you want Marcus's old uniform for?"

I took a deep breath and swallowed any emotion before turning to look up at her.

"Tomorrow after lunch I'm going to be a Sheldon Sea Turtle."

Chapter Fourteen

On Monday I awoke to a bugle playing reveille in my ear. It was the military's morning wake-up call, which meant only one person could be pacing the floor beside my bed.

"I'm up, I'm up." I swatted at the CD player blasting the music, but Major held it just out of my reach.

"Do you have any idea what time it is?"

I checked my alarm clock, which read 6:53. "I still have an hour until school starts. Don't worry. I'll be on time."

Major finally turned off the CD

player. "Your mother tells me that on mornings when the school paper comes out, you're already in class by now to help with the final layout."

Ordinarily, this was true, but ordinarily, I wouldn't have spent the weekend before kissing my editor and assaulting my co-reporter with turbo-strength apple pie spice.

"I turned my articles in last night. Ben doesn't need my help to put the *Bugle* together." I shrugged and added a yawn for good measure.

Major scrutinized me. "You're a creature of habit, Delilah, and I know this paper is important to you. I refuse to believe you've suddenly taken less of an interest." He narrowed his eyes. "Which means something's changed."

"Everything's the same." I burrowed under the blankets. "I just don't want to share the front page with the French girl." It wasn't a complete lie, but it would be enough to keep Major from getting suspicious.

"And sleeping in will get you what you want?"

"No, but I can *dream* that it will." My words were muffled by several inches of blanket, which Major pulled down until he could see my face.

"You have to *fight* for what you believe in, Delilah."

As much as I hated to admit it, his sappy made-for-TV moral was true. My weekend drama might have been more than enough reason to avoid school until everyone graduated, but I needed to be there to keep an eye on Ava. If people started to think I didn't care about the paper, I could kiss the front page good-bye.

Thirty minutes later, I walked through the front doors of the school to find Paige and Jenner waiting for me. Jenner looked pained, as if she'd been listening to one of Paige's beauty rants, and the first thing she did was tackle me with a hug.

"She's trying to convince me that blue eye shadow will make me a better surfer. Make her stop!"

Paige didn't respond, but I could sense her hovering around me. "What?" I finally turned, only to catch her staring aghast at my outfit.

"Your debut edition comes out today, you're the hot topic of the school, and you dress like *that*?"

Jenner rolled her eyes, but this time I couldn't disagree with Paige. My outfit was designed to help me blend in with the uniformed crowd at Sheldon, not win any beauty contests. I'd borrowed one of my mom's navy blue business skirts, which was one of Sheldon's colors, and paired it with a plain white button-up shirt and black Mary Janes.

"You look like a flight attendant!" Paige reached into her bag. "But I can fix that with scissors and a little glitter glue."

I grabbed her hand. "*Don't* even try. I need this skirt to be perfectly boring to fit in at Sheldon."

Her fingers flew to my waist and started rolling up the skirt. "At least wear something that shows your knees. And tie this around your neck." She fished a silk scarf out of her bag, knotted it around my collar, and stepped back to inspect her handiwork. "Much less frightening, but the shoes could still use a little pizzazz." She smiled hopefully and reached for her glitter glue.

"Absolutely not."

The three of us made our way down the hall, and I kept my eyes fixed on the lockers. If people were pointing and whispering, I didn't want to know. Unfortunately, I was so focused on ignoring everyone that I didn't even see Marcus until he was standing right in front of me.

"Marcus!" I yelped, startled. He jumped too, along with Jenner and Paige.

Paige took Jenner's sleeve and pulled her far enough away to allow Marcus and me to talk, but close enough so she could still hear everything.

"Here." Marcus dropped a navy blue sweater emblazoned with the Sheldon crest into my arms. "Good luck with whatever you're planning."

"Thank you." He walked away, and I clutched the sweater to my chest, the scent of detergent wafting upward. "You . . . you didn't have to wash it," I called after him.

He turned and shrugged. "It smelled like me."

My nose buried in the sweater, I summoned up the courage to say, "I don't mind the way you smell."

Paige clapped a hand to her forehead, so I assumed it hadn't been the *best* compliment to give a guy, but Marcus didn't seem to mind.

Smiling, he ran his fingers through his hair and came back over. "I . . . uh . . . meant that people would get suspicious if you walked past them smelling like a guy."

"Oh." I wondered if the pink in my cheeks clashed with the Sheldon blue. "Well, thanks again."

Instead of leaving, Marcus shifted his weight from foot to foot. "So, I hope the sweater isn't *too* big."

I tried it on. The sleeves engulfed my hands, and the bottom hung just below *my* bottom. "It's a little huge, but that's okay." I started to take it off. "If anyone asks, I can say it belongs to my boyf—" I froze with the sweater halfway around my head.

"Boyfriend," Jenner completed for me. Then she squealed in pain and rounded on Paige. "Why'd you pinch me?"

Paige regarded her with wide eyes. "You're embarrassing Delilah."

Jenner's forehead wrinkled. "Because I said the word 'boyfriend'? It's not as if she *likes* . . ." She turned to point at Marcus and saw the mortified look on my face, "Um . . ."

No sweater was big enough to hide me at that moment.

"It's not as if she likes who?" Marcus pretended to not understand, but the corners of his eyes were crinkling, and he was staring intently in my direction.

I cleared my throat and checked my watch. "Wow. Look at the time. Thanks again for the sweater. You'll have it back by the end of the day."

Without even waiting for Jenner or Paige, I hurried to my locker. From a distance the locker looked like it was spotted with red polka dots, and when I reached it, I discovered why.

The entire surface was covered in lipstick kisses. I opened the door and an avalanche of Styrofoam peanuts quivered and tumbled over the front of my clothes and onto the floor. Static electricity caused the packing bits to stick to me, and I noticed that each one had a word written on it in French. Somehow I doubted any of them were nice.

Two kids from my math class stood nearby, watching me empty books into my locker and murmuring to each other.

"Who do you think she'll go after next?"

"You don't think she'll keep chasing Ben?"

"Well, he rejected her, so she's probably on the prowl. Whose sweater is she holding?"

I glared at them, kicking my way through the Styrofoam. "You might want to learn the true meaning of 'whisper.'" The closest one winced as I approached her. "And keep an eye on your boyfriends . . . because I'm on the prowl!" I waggled my fingers in her face and stormed off to the journalism room.

Ben sat alone at the table, articles spread out before him, and he glanced up when he heard me move through the doorway. He didn't look thrilled.

I stopped a few feet from the table. "Hey."

He nodded and returned to his work. "Hey."

His response hadn't included any mean names or rude gestures, so it was a safe bet that he didn't hate me nearly as much as his girlfriend did.

I let out a deep breath and took a tentative step toward him. "On a scale of one to five million, how mad are you?"

He answered but didn't look at me. "Depends. Are you talking about the fact that you kissed me, the fact that you brought my enemy to the social, or the fact that you nearly blinded my girlfriend?"

My fingers twisted themselves into a knot. "All of the above?" I dropped into a chair beside him and the papers fluttered, threatening to slide to the floor.

Ben lunged for them. "Zero, five million, and zero." When I looked at him curiously, he explained, "I wasn't mad that you kissed me. Just . . . shocked. And I know you didn't spray Ava on purpose."

I bowed my head. "But you weren't a fan of Marcus being there."

Ben leaned back in his chair and sighed. "You know how much I hate him. You know the kind of guy he used to be."

"*Used* to be," I repeated. "He's changed . . . just like you've changed."

"Don't compare me to *him*, and don't ever, *ever* bring him around me again." Ben must have realized how harsh he sounded, because he rested a hand on my arm. "You and I will always be friends, but you'll never convince me to like the guy."

"You don't have to." I fixed my eyes on his. "Because . . . because *I* do."

I'd finally voiced the words to someone, and the earth hadn't exploded.

Ben and I stared at each other for a moment, and then he nodded and pulled away. "I could tell from your article." He waved the paper and smiled. "You did a pretty good job of making Marcus sound like a halfway normal person."

"That's because he *is*."

Ben shrugged, and I knew I would never win that battle with him. At least we'd come to an understanding.

"Okay, then . . ." I returned my article to the table and gave him a sly grin. "Do you need help deciding which piece goes front and center?"

"Nobody's going to believe that's your real hair." Jenner sat on the restroom counter while I adjusted the blond wig I'd found in the drama department's wardrobe. It was ten minutes into lunch, the only time the restroom was devoid of all female life, and I was dressing up for my espionage adventure at Sheldon.

"Redheads stand out anywhere," I informed her.

"So do blondes who look like their hair was gnawed by rats." Jenner tried to run a comb through the snarls of the wig, but it immediately became entangled and ripped the wig off my head. I caught it before it hit the floor, almost busting a seam in my mom's skirt in the process.

"It's fine. Nobody will notice." I put the wig back on and smoothed it down.

"You're right. They'll be too busy wondering if you're a deflated bodybuilder." She tugged on the baggy sleeve of the Sheldon sweater. "This isn't going to work, Delilah."

"Of course it will. It has to." I checked my reflection in the mirror, then headed for the door.

Leaving the school turned out to be easier than I had planned. I caught a city bus across town and got off half a block from the Sheldon campus, with five minutes until the end of lunch. The night before, I'd printed out the school's schedule and building map so I'd be able to blend in . . . despite my rat-eaten wig.

Giving the wig one more smoothing, I walked around the school until I'd reached the rear courtyard where students ate lunch. A few of them glanced up when they saw me, but if they thought anything seemed unusual, they kept it to themselves. I weaved among the tables in search of the one face I'd been picturing since the night before . . . the editor of the *Sheldon Sentinel*, Henry Cho. Unfortunately, as kids started filing into the building, he wasn't among them, which meant he'd either eaten inside or was working on *his* newspaper.

I followed the crowd into the school and tried my best to not gawk *too* much at the decorations and banners on the walls. Sheldon's journalism room was across from the library, but when I peered through the window, the room was dark. I hurried up the hall to the eighth-grade lockers, but again, Henry Cho was nowhere to be found.

A nagging doubt tugged at the back of my mind— maybe Henry wasn't even at school. I hadn't thought to look up anyone else on the newspaper staff, so if I couldn't find him, my whole trip would be pointless. My only hope was to sneak into the journalism room and find the information on my own.

The halls were starting to empty, and I had to duck into several doorways to avoid teachers doing last-minute sweeps for stragglers. When the warning bell rang, I pushed open the door to the journalism room and dropped to my hands and knees as their shadows passed by the windows. After a few minutes I flipped open my cell phone and used it to light my way across the room to a bookshelf filled with year-books. I found the one for the previous year and flipped slowly through the pages, looking for mention of the fire or pictures of Katie.

Suddenly the lights flipped on.

I froze, lifting my head to see who'd caught me.

An Asian guy with a shock of spiky black hair and a cute but crooked smile stood in the doorway. "It's easier to find what you're looking for with the lights on," he said.

I dropped the yearbook and got to my feet, brushing off my skirt. "You're Henry, right?"

"I am." He continued to show his pearly whites as he picked up the book. "You must be new."

"Actually"—I reached behind him to close the door—"I'm from Brighton Academy. I came to ask you something."

Henry's smile finally fell. "You came from Brighton?"

"Yes. I snuck out of there and into here."

"What!?" Henry clapped a hand to his mouth. "Get out! You snuck into our school?"

"Yes," I said, still not sure if he would help me or rat me out. "I need to know about one of the students who used to go here."

Henry's stunned expression turned into a curious one. "Who are you interested in?"

"Katie Glenn."

He raised his eyebrows. "She's not torching *your* class-rooms, is she?"

I couldn't help the excited gasp that escaped me. "So, she *did* start the fire in the science lab!"

Henry tilted his head to one side and glanced thought-fully at the ceiling. "Well . . . she never confessed to it, but that's what everyone thinks. Even the police."

"The police?" I shook my head in confusion. "The papers said it was an unsolved case."

Henry leaned toward me. "Because they were *paid* to say that . . . and the papers and the school were paid to stay quiet too." When I glanced at him doubtfully, he crossed his heart. "I would've broken the story if I could've."

I pulled up two chairs and dropped into one of them. "Have a seat. I want to know everything."

"Okay." Henry sat obediently and opened the yearbook he was holding. "The thing is . . . you have to know the old Katie first."

Chapter Fifteen

A purple-haired girl wearing a cutoff T-shirt stuck her tongue out at me . . . or rather, at the person taking the photo.

Student by day, rebel by night, the caption said.

I stared at the image in disbelief. *"That's* Katie?"

Henry took the yearbook from me and flipped through to another page. "Here she is again."

This time Katie wore her school uniform but was holding a lit match in each hand and smirking at the camera.

Mess with fire and you're gonna get burned, the caption said.

I shot Henry a dubious look. "Nobody suspected anything even after seeing this?"

"The 'tough' students used to do that for fun," he said. "They'd light matches and have contests to see who could hold on the longest. Katie was one of the best."

I leaned back in thought. "Did she have easy access to matches?"

Henry shook his head. "The school banned them way before the fire. Although, knowing her, she probably still carried some."

"She is *so* different now." I traced the edge of the picture. "I could never imagine her looking like this."

"The Friday before the fire, her hair was longer than yours," he explained, marking a spot halfway down his back, "but the following Monday"—he held his hand up by his ears—"suddenly she was one of the guys."

I tapped the yearbook with my finger. "She also used to wear T-shirts like in that other picture. But she *never* wears them anymore."

Henry shivered. "You don't want her to. After the fire she wore these heavy bandages on her arms for weeks and told everybody it was because she had had an allergic reaction to something."

"But she burned them in the fire." I smacked myself on the forehead. That explained her obsession with keeping her arms covered. She didn't want anyone to see the scars.

Henry nodded. "Her hair too."

Katie's little quirks were starting to make more sense, but I still wasn't sure how the fire extinguisher came into play and why she'd allowed herself to get burned. People who started fires usually didn't get caught in them.

I turned to Henry. "Is it possible she set the place on fire by accident?"

He gave me a thumbs-down. "The police never told the papers, but they found an accelerant in the chem lab."

"A what?"

"You know, something to make the fire spread faster."

"Then . . . whoever set the fire did it on purpose." I frowned and told him about the extinguisher in Katie's locker.

"Maybe she's afraid of fire now," he said, "and keeps it in her locker just in case."

I mulled this over and shook my head. "She was sitting by a bonfire on the beach last week, and her new clique is called Hot Stuff. Does that sound like someone who's afraid?"

Henry narrowed his eyes and gazed off into the distance. "What are her new friends like? Bad girls?"

"They're rude, shallow—pretty much any snob stereotype you can think of. But definitely not bad. Katie made it clear she doesn't hang out with people like that."

He took the yearbook back from me and turned to the student portrait section. "These were her best friends, the Harper twins." He pointed to side-by-side pictures of scowling sisters, both with wrinkled blouses, one sporting a black eye. "*They* were bad girls."

The more I learned about the old Katie, the more I realized she was trying very hard to be the complete opposite of who she once had been. She seemed to be ashamed of her past, but I didn't understand the sudden change of heart.

"Listen." Henry shifted in his chair. "I hate to say this, but I really have some stories to prep."

"Sure." I got to my feet. "Thanks for all your help."

He smiled. "I just hope you can get a confession out of her. *That* would make a great story."

I felt a thrill go up my spine. "It would, wouldn't it?"

"Totally." He nodded confidently and winked. "We're talking Junior Global Journalist–worthy."

"Yeah . . ." I wandered out the door and down the hall, already envisioning the article in my head. It was too late to make it into the debut edition of the paper, but I could definitely have it ready for next week if I could just get Katie to tell me the story herself. Hopefully, after the article on Marcus, she'd be convinced *and* I could include pictures of the damage from the original fire.

"Excuse me, miss!" a man's voice called out.

This was why I never daydreamed. Startled, I stumbled a little over the carpet. Patting my head to make sure my wig was secure, I turned toward him, smiling.

"Yes, sir?"

He crossed one arm over his chest and held out the other, palm up. "Hall pass, please."

"Oh! Um . . . I think it's here somewhere." I checked the pockets of my mom's skirt thoroughly. The man looked fairly old. If I stood there long enough, he might forget why he stopped me or fall asleep. It happened to my grandparents all the time.

Sadly, the man wasn't as elderly as his white hair implied. He stood there, alert and watching me with hawklike eyes. "Well?"

"I must have dropped it." I giggled and shrugged. "Back to class I go."

The man pointed down the hall, and for a second, I thought I was in the clear. Then I realized he was pointing at the headmaster's office. "Nice try."

I tried a different approach. "You know, the headmaster said that if I got in trouble one more time, he'd send me home. Why don't I just go there now and you can tell him I'm sorry?" I made a move toward the courtyard, but the man clamped a hand on my shoulder.

"Sweetheart, I *am* the headmaster."

I blushed and faced him. "Oh! Then . . . I can tell you in person."

The headmaster scratched his chin. "The funny thing is, I've never told a student I would send them home."

"Well"—I cleared my throat—"there's always a first time."

He squinted at me. "And I've never met a student who didn't recognize me."

I looked him up and down. "Well, you've . . . uh . . . changed since the last time I saw you. Have you been losing weight?"

"Let's go, funny girl." The headmaster steered me toward his office and snatched the book bag out of my hand before I could stop him. "Brighton Junior Academy. I wonder if they've missed you." He raised an eyebrow at me. "Or if they're even aware you're gone."

"Oh, they know." I opened the door and stepped into his office. "They just don't know I came here."

The headmaster handed the bag back. "What's your name?"

Now I faced a dilemma.

If I told the truth, I'd be in serious trouble with my headmaster and Major.

If I lied, I'd have to use the name of a real Brighton

student, and when the Sheldon headmaster found out I was lying, I'd be in serious trouble with him, *my* headmaster, Major, and whatever kid I pretended to be.

If I didn't say anything, the Sheldon headmaster would be forced to keep me in his office, going over the list of absent students with my headmaster. With the blond wig they'd never come to the conclusion it was me, which would buy me time to come up with an escape plan . . . unless the Sheldon headmaster got fed up and drove me back to Brighton. Then I would be back where I started.

My options were bleak, but staying silent seemed the most promising, so when the Sheldon headmaster asked my name a second time, I just blinked up at him.

He sighed and directed me to sit in a chair opposite his desk. "You know I'll figure out who you are sooner or later."

"I'm hoping later," I answered.

He shook his head and turned to his computer, while I settled back with my hands in my pockets. With as little movement as possible, I opened my cell phone and cupped it in my palm. Since I'd had the phone for two years, I knew the buttons blindfolded, so I sent a 911 text message to Jenner. Then I started squirming in my seat. "Uh-oh."

The headmaster glanced at me. "What seems to be the problem?"

I held my stomach and bent forward. "I think I'm gonna be sick."

He looked at me suspiciously, but the moment my hand flew up to my mouth, he pointed to a side door. "Please! Go . . . uh . . . use the faculty restroom."

Nodding, I got to my feet and hurried through the door with my bag hidden under one arm. It led to a hallway that branched into the teacher's lounge. My phone buzzed in my hand, and I ducked into the restroom, locking the door behind me.

"Okay, it can't be that bad," said Jenner. "You answered your phone."

"I got sent to the headmaster's office!" I whispered back. "At a school I don't even go to."

She sucked in her breath. "That *is* bad. How tight are the shackles?"

I glanced around the restroom. "The . . . huh?"

"They've got you chained up somewhere, right? Some secret room behind the janitor's closet, where all the bad children are sent?"

I slapped my hand to my forehead in frustration. "I should have texted Paige."

"Hey!" Jenner squealed in protest. "Would you rather have help from someone who remembers the escape scenes from hundreds of horror movies or someone who'd

175

recommend you reapply your makeup while you wait to die?"

She had a point. "So, how do I get out of here? I'm trapped in the bathroom right now."

The phone went quiet for a moment. "I have a brilliant plan. Are there any windows?"

"No."

"Get someplace with windows," she said, "and then climb out."

"That's your brilliant plan?" I hissed. "Go out the window?" Nevertheless, I slowly opened the bathroom door and peeked into the hall. The door to the headmaster's office was still closed, so I crept toward the teacher's lounge. It was empty and brightly lit by sunshine pouring through several windows.

"I'm in escape heaven," I told Jenner. "Hang on." I cradled the phone against my shoulder and unlocked the first window. Just as I started to ease it open, Jenner cried, "No, wait! There—"

An ear-splitting siren drowned out her last words as an alarm above the window announced my escape.

"No!" I lifted the window the rest of the way and shoved my bag through before hoisting myself up.

"Go!" cried Jenner. "Go, go, go!"

Pocketing my phone, I scrambled up and out over the

hedges surrounding the school, feeling my wig tear away from my head in the process.

With the biggest part of my disguise gone, I tugged the sweater over my real hair so just my face peeked out. I could only imagine what I looked like—a headless girl tearing across the school lawn in a business skirt.

As soon as I reached the faculty parking lot, I pulled the phone out of my pocked and dialed Jenner.

"Did you get away?" she asked.

"Barely," I panted into the phone. "Do you have any extra clothes I can borrow when I get back to school? I have a feeling the headmaster will try to ID me by my outfit."

I turned to glance back at the school. Nobody was following me, but I couldn't risk someone chasing after me in their car. I kept running.

"I have the clothes I wear for gym," said Jenner. "But I can't guarantee they smell so great."

"That's fine." The entrance to the school opened onto a busy street. On the opposite side was a bus stop. "I'll be there in fifteen minutes. Meet me by the gym."

I spent the entire bus ride fidgeting with the sleeves of Marcus's sweater and glancing out the window, like a convicted felon on the run. Thankfully, no police cars tailed the bus, and when I reached Brighton, no headmaster waited on the front lawn to drag me inside and shackle me in a secret room.

Down at the gym, Jenner handed me a pair of ripped brown cargo shorts and a purple T-shirt with a massive bleach stain on the shoulder. While I changed, I filled her in on what I'd learned.

"Wow. That should definitely be enough to take down Hot Stuff," she said. "When are you going to tell Paige?"

"After I have one more talk with Katie. I'd like to get a good story out of this if I can." I studied my reflection in the mirror. "I'm not a fashion snob, but shouldn't you have thrown these clothes out by now?"

She shrugged. "If I'd known you'd need them to double as a disguise one day, I would have chosen better." She handed me a pair of Converses that were two sizes too big and the perfect finishing touch for my clown costume.

"How do I look?" I struck a few poses.

"Like you could give Paige a heart attack." Jenner grabbed my hand. "Come on. The paper's already out."

"It is?" I gave a little squeal and sped my walk, dragging her behind me. "Why didn't you bring me a copy?"

Jenner grinned. "I wanted you to grab one off the *news rack* yourself."

I gasped and gripped her arms. "There's a news rack?"

"Mrs. Bradford wanted it to be a surprise. It's outside the journalism room."

For a moment, I forgot all about Sheldon and Katie and the heaps of trouble I'd be in if anyone could trace the blond wig back to me. I let go of Jenner's hand and half galloped, half ran to the gleaming metal box piled high with neatly folded papers.

I opened the box, grabbed the top copy, and took a deep inhale of fresh ink. My heart beat a little faster as I snapped the paper open and scanned the page for my stories.

And right at the very top, there it was. My first headline of the year.

"'Marcus Taylor,'" I read aloud to Jenner, grinning. "'The Boy Behind the Bandit, by Ava Pi—'"

My stomach dropped into the toes of Jenner's old Converses. My throat locked up and refused to produce any more sound, leaving my mouth to flap open and closed like a dying fish.

"By *who*?" Jenner snatched the paper from me and clapped a hand to her mouth. "Delilah, no!"

My body started to tremble, first in my knees and continuing upward until I reached a shaking hand out to take the paper back from Jenner.

Maybe Ava had written an article about him too. Maybe she'd only taken my title and attached it to her own work. I read the first few lines, but they blurred before my eyes as my hand shook even harder and tears clouded my vision.

The story was mine.

"She stole my work," I whispered.

Chapter Sixteen

Y ou have to tell Mrs. Bradford about this." Jenner gave me a tissue and a hug. "This whole nightmare's been going on too long."

I just blubbered into the tissue and shook my head.

Jenner sighed. "Delilah, this little war with Ava is getting serious. One of you needs to stop it, and if you tell Mrs. Bradford, she can send out a correction in the next issue *and* punish Ava."

"It won't matter," I squeaked. "The damage is done."

Someone gasped behind us, and I turned to see Paige running toward me, hand pressed to her forehead. "What *happened*?"

"Ava stole my article." I sniffled.

Paige shook her head. "I meant your outfit. It's like my worst nightmare come true!"

Jenner pushed her. "*Not* helping. Can't you see Delilah's in pain?"

I handed Paige the newspaper, and she frowned. "How did Ava steal your article? Your name's right here." She jabbed at the piece I'd written on Jenner.

"No!" I moaned. "I'm talking about the one on Marcus."

"Oh!" She studied the page for a moment. "Your writing's much better in this one."

The crying must have clouded my brain. Was the girl who could barely read really criticizing my journalism skills?

"What are you talking about?" I asked.

"Well, I'm pretty sure 'surfer' doesn't have a 'ph' in it. And you have a lot of sentences that just stop mid-thought."

I lowered her hand so I could read the Jenner interview. Sure enough, the entire article looked as if it had been written by a third grader.

"Arghhhh!" I took the front page and ripped it into a thousand pieces. "That's not what I turned in! That little . . ." I launched into a slew of insults that would *never* be allowed in any article.

"Tell Mrs. Bradford," Jenner repeated. "I'm sure she can clear up the whole thing."

I grabbed a fresh copy of the paper off the news rack and stormed into the journalism room, where Ben was already talking with Mrs. Bradford. When they saw me, they both spoke at once.

"I don't know what happened," said Ben.

"We can have it corrected next week," said Mrs. Bradford.

I threw the paper onto the table and pointed to Ben. "I can tell you *exactly* what happened. Your girlfriend put her name on my Marcus article and ruined my Jenner article to get back at me for Saturday."

Mrs. Bradford stepped closer and put a hand on my arm. "I'm sure that's not the case. No member of the paper would deliberately do something like that. It was an accident."

"No, it wasn't!" I shouted. "You have to get this fixed today!"

Mrs. Bradford folded her hands and brought them to her lips. "Delilah, I think you're overreacting a little. This isn't that big of a deal."

Ben nodded. "And I know Ava. She would never hurt anyone."

I just stared at them both, unable to form a single sentence that wouldn't include the words "you" and "suck."

Ben took my silence as a chance to add, "It's just the first issue. You can get it right the next time."

If I'd had superpowers, Ben would have been nothing but a pile of ashes. "Get it right the *next time*? There was nothing wrong with it the first time!" Turning on my heel, I left the room, slamming the door behind me.

"So . . . maybe telling Mrs. Bradford wasn't a good idea," said Jenner.

I shook my head, running both hands through my hair. "She won't help me. She—" I paused at the sound of an annoyingly familiar French voice, coming from around the corner.

"You are too kind," said Ava. "My article was good, but not *wonderful.*"

"It really was," a girl's voice insisted. "I never knew Marcus until I read your work."

My eyes widened, and I gaped at Jenner and Paige.

Ava laughed. "Well, thank you. I wanted to give him a chance after that cruel article Delilah James wrote about him last year. I thought it would make him feel better to know *someone* at the school treats him like a person."

I sputtered for a moment and lunged forward to poke Ava's eyes out with my pencil, but Jenner and Paige each took one of my arms.

"You're only going to make this worse," whispered Jenner.

"Ava might claw you," whispered Paige. "And you can't risk facial trauma before the Debutante selection."

On the other side of the wall, Ava continued to brag. "People said the Swirlie Bandit could never be tamed. . . ."

"His name is *Marcus*," I growled under my breath.

"But I guess he just needed to meet the right girl," Ava finished.

"You're amazing," said someone else, a guy this time. "I thought you'd hate him after he fought your boyfriend Saturday night."

I gave Jenner and Paige a smug smile. I couldn't wait to see how Ava answered *that*.

Without skipping a beat, she purred, "I know it was not his fault. He was just too distraught at being forced to take Delilah to the social."

"What?!" The word exploded from my lips before I could stop it. Shaking off Jenner and Paige, I stormed around the corner and into Ava's face. "I did *not* force him to go with me, and you did *not* write that article." I pointed at a copy of the paper she was holding. "I did!"

Ava turned to the guy and girl with her and smirked. "Of course, Delilah. You wrote it. Whatever you say."

The guy and girl shook their heads piteously at me.

"She did!" Jenner stepped up beside me. "She even made Marcus go to the social with her so . . ." She faltered under

Ava's triumphant gaze. "I mean . . . she didn't *make* him."

I closed my eyes and groaned. "Jenner."

"You are a horrible person," the girl with Ava said to me in disgust. "First, you try and steal Ava's boyfriend, then you try and steal her *article*?"

"It was *my* article!" With an enraged growl I grabbed Jenner's arm and hauled her away. After what had happened Saturday, everyone was on Ava's side. There was no point in trying to talk through the matter.

It was time for action.

I let go of Jenner once we were back with Paige and headed for the entrance to the school.

"Where are you going?" Jenner and Paige hurried to catch up to me.

"To see Major. You're right. I need to put a stop to this once and for all."

"Telling Mrs. Bradford didn't do anything. What makes you think telling your stepdad will help?" asked Paige.

"He works in military defense," I said. "If anyone knows how to take down the enemy, he does."

To say Major was thrilled to see me would have been less of a slight exaggeration and more of a total lie. The minute I walked into the lobby of the defense building, he frowned.

"I'm confused. You don't appear to be missing any limbs

or coughing up blood, but you're still out of school." He leaned away and took in my outfit. "And what happened to the clothes you were wearing this morning?"

I patted my backpack. "They're in here. And I'm out of school because of a project I'm working on." I recited the speech I'd been practicing the entire bus ride. "My teacher gave us time for independent study, so I'm using mine to get help from you."

Major raised one eyebrow. "I'm sure she meant for you to study on campus, Delilah."

I smiled up at him and batted my eyelashes. "But you're better than any textbook. You're like a walking library."

Major narrowed his eyes, then steered me toward the receptionist's window. "Could we get a visitor's badge for Delilah James?" To me, he said, "Don't think you've flattered me into agreement. I plan to use your words against you in the future."

I nodded and clipped on the badge. "Just like any other parent."

The receptionist buzzed us back into the secure area of the building, and Major pointed to his office, a large room that looked more like a storage unit. Shelves of assorted junk lined every wall, and a desk in the far corner struggled to keep the chaos in order.

"Don't ever let your room get like this," said Major.

"What *is* all this stuff?" I asked, picking up a plastic package with the word "Meal" on it.

"Some of them are prototypes for devices. Others are random items left behind by the captain who had this office before me." Major took the package from me. "This is an MRE, Meal Ready-to-Eat. Be lucky I don't serve these to you at home."

He returned it to the shelf. "But let's get back to your project. What sort of information are you looking for?"

"My project's on warfare, so I just need to know how to end a war." I pulled my spiral notepad and a pen out of my backpack and waited for his answer.

"How to . . ." Major laughed so loud, the pen jumped from my fingers and clattered to the floor. "Delilah, there's no simple answer to a question like that."

"But wars always end at some point." I stooped to pick up my pen. "How?"

Major shook his head. "If you want the simple solution, which there *never* is," he repeated, "wars end in three ways." He counted them off on his fingers. "You win, you lose, or you come to a truce."

I frowned. No amount of strapless dresses or froufrou fashion would convince Ava to just shake hands and leave it all behind us, and I would *never* admit defeat to her. "Okay. Um . . . how do you win a war, then?"

He smiled and walked toward a dry erase board covered with notes and dates. "*That* is even more difficult than ending a war." He erased the top half of the notes. "But you start with the basics. Number one being deception." He jotted on the board. "You trick the enemy into thinking your actions serve a different purpose than they actually do."

"Serve . . . different purpose . . . than . . . actual." I wrote down what he said and then looked up, perplexed. "Huh?"

"For example . . ." He tapped his pen against his chin. "Say a man on the boardwalk comes up to you and starts juggling. While you're watching him, his partner steals your purse. You thought the juggler was there to entertain you, but he was really there to distract you from the robbery."

"Ohhh."

Major returned to the board. "The second winning strategy is to attack your enemy's weakest point. Hit them close to home."

That needed no explanation. I knew Ava's weakest point.

"You can also find someone else, an ally, to fight your battle for you."

I shook my head. "I want to do this alone."

Major stopped writing and faced me. "What?"

My eyes widened. "I mean . . . if I . . . was in a war. I'd want to fight my own battle. What else do you have?"

He regarded me for a moment more, then turned back to the board. "Number four, strike when morale is low." He cleared his throat. "In other words, kick them when they're down."

"Gotcha."

"And finally, we come to the element of surprise, which can completely stun an enemy and leave him open for attack." He underlined the last point and put down the marker. "Any questions?"

I put down my pen as well and thought for a moment. While Major had been talking, I'd been thinking about how I could incorporate his rules into an attack on Ava. I'd need a few supplies, but unfortunately, I was low on funds. "Can I have an advance on my allowance?"

Major smirked. "Any questions about what I've written on the board?"

"Oh. No, I think this is a good start." I gave him a hopeful smile. "But I'd still like some money . . . for school supplies."

"I don't suppose I can deny those." He reached for his wallet. "What are you planning to buy exactly?"

"Just some highlighters, spiral notepads, pens. About twenty dollars' worth of stuff."

Major counted out the money and handed it over. "Before you go, I want you to take some books home." He crossed the room and browsed a shelf crammed full of hardbacks. "Have you ever heard of *The Art of War?*" He disappeared behind the shelf and kept searching.

"No," I said, trying to keep the dismay out of my voice. My fake project was suddenly leading to a lot of real work, and somehow I had a feeling that *The Art of War* was more of a sleep aid than a good read.

While I waited for Major to emerge with some twenty-pound backbreaker, I leaned against one of the shelves. Something smacked the floor by my feet, and I jumped, looking down to see the MRE package.

"Hey, Major? Can I open this MRE thing?"

"Help yourself!" he called.

I picked it up and ripped into the bag, astounded by all the contents: ravioli, cookies, crackers, and cheese spread—it even came with a tiny bottle of hot sauce. The only thing missing was a toothbrush and toothpaste to clean up afterward. Though I supposed toothpaste would just make a sticky mess.

I dropped the crackers and let out a gasp, struck full-force by my own brilliance.

Toothpaste *would* be a sticky mess. A sticky, embarrassing, almost-impossible-to-wash-off mess. The grand finale to my master plan.

I put all the MRE items back into the bag and joined

Major. "I'm sure what you told me should be enough. I don't really need any books."

"Don't be silly." He loaded my arms with books until I resembled a teen hunchback. "You'll need a reliable source for your information, and *that* comes from *these*." He dusted his hands off and placed them on his hips. "Now, is there anything else?"

"Not unless you have a wheelbarrow," I grunted. The top book shifted and I maneuvered the stack to keep it from falling, almost tripping over my own feet.

"You'll be fine." Major moved to clap me on the back, then thought better of it. "A little hard work never killed anyone."

"How about books? Have they ever killed anyone?"

He nudged me toward the door. "Head straight home, all right? I'll see you in about an hour."

"Okay." I leaned against the door and readjusted my grip. "But if I'm not there, look for me on the side of the road. I'll probably be buried under these."

The walk to the bus stop was painful, and it involved a great deal of sweating in Jenner's gym clothes, which released a crowd-scattering odor. When I finally climbed onto the bus, I dreaded the moment it would pull up to my stop . . . until I saw Marcus waiting there.

Chapter Seventeen

Mixed emotions of happiness and hor- ror coursed through me. On the one hand, I was about to bump into him. On the other hand, I smelled like a mule farmer. Ducking low in my seat, I said a prayer to the gods of public indecency and pulled off my shirt, trading it for Marcus's sweater. There was no way I could get into the skirt without extreme embarrassment, so I simply hoped Marcus would be too tall for the stink of Jenner's pants to reach him.

Running my fingers through my hair, I slung my bag over one shoulder, grabbed the mountain of books, and walked off the bus in a cool, calm manner. When Marcus saw me, he smiled and got up.

"Hey, Delilah. I was starting to think you'd never show up."

"You were waiting for me?" My heart fluttered, and my hand went up to play with my hair. Unfortunately, one of the heavier books had pinned my sleeve down, so when I lifted my arm, the top half of the stack tumbled to the sidewalk. "Ugh!"

Marcus stooped and grabbed the books but didn't hand them to me. "Yeah. I thought I'd walk you home and we could talk about your trip to Sheldon." He tugged at the sweater. "Just out of curiosity, why are you still wearing this?"

I glanced down and blushed. "Oh! Um . . . it's just really comfortable and I'm a little chilly."

His forehead wrinkled. "You look like you've been sweating buckets. Maybe you have a fever."

I wiped at my face with the sleeve. "No. I was just really nervous breaking into Sheldon." Suddenly I realized how gross I must have looked, using his sweater like a sponge, and I lowered my arm. "Sorry. I'll wash this and get it back to you."

"No hurry," he said. "So, how *was* Sheldon? Did you"—he waggled his eyebrows—"uncover the truth?"

"Of course." I started walking toward my street. "And

it was *very* juicy . . . but you already knew that."

He nodded and listened while I explained everything I'd learned.

"You should talk to Katie, you know," he said when I finished. "Before you talk to Paige."

"I'm going to," I said. "Maybe I can get her to do an interview with me like you did."

Marcus nudged my arm. "I wanted to talk to you about that, too. That article you wrote was great."

I rolled my eyes. "You mean the one *Ava* wrote?"

"Yeah," he winced. "Sorry about that. But you know you wrote it, and *I* know you wrote it, and I've been telling people that whenever they talk to me."

"You have?" I looked up at him in surprise. Ben's response to my distress had been to do nothing, but Marcus had made an effort to set things straight on his own. If my arms hadn't been about to fall off, I would have hugged him.

"Thank you," I said. Then the rest of his words sank in. "Wait. People have been going up to you?"

"Yeah." He grinned. "They keep telling me they never knew what I'd been going through and that they've felt the same way, and that they're so sorry. Then I say that *I'm* sorry for any trouble I caused, and the girls cry, and the guys punch me in the arm." He shifted his portion of the books to one side and squeezed my shoulders. "And it's all because of you.

That article might be the greatest thing you've ever written."

His compliment should have made me happy, but I couldn't get the image of Ava's name attached to *my* work out of my mind.

"The greatest thing"—I shrugged him off—"that people are giving her credit for!"

Marcus stared at me in bewilderment. "Why are you upset? I told you I've been fixing it."

"You don't understand. This was the first issue of the year and a *huge* article, and no matter what you say, people are still going to remember Ava's name when they think about it. Plus, she has this lie she's been telling people about why she wrote it that makes me look like a jerk."

"So what?" He waved a dismissive hand. "This is school. It's not the rest of your life."

I glared at him. "Says the guy who made me write the article so everyone would like him."

Instead of getting furious, Marcus blushed and lowered his eyes. "I don't need everyone to like me. Just you."

"Oh," I said. He had discovered the quickest way to soothe an angry girl's temper—blatant flattery. "What?"

"Don't get me wrong," he said. "I'm still happy that people aren't treating me like a mutant anymore, but whenever you don't like me, it makes me feel a hundred times worse than anyone else does."

"Well," I cleared my throat. "Well . . . I . . ." I licked my lips. "I like you right *now*."

Marcus smiled. "And that makes me feel a hundred times better."

We reached my front yard and he walked with me up to the porch.

"Thanks for your help," I told him. "And . . . I'll see you tomorrow." I gave him a polite nod, unsure of how to handle things, since we'd just admitted our feelings but weren't yet officially . . . anything.

"Sure. Let me just give you these." Marcus loaded the books he was carrying back into my arms. "And this . . ." While I was busy trying to shuffle them into my pile, he reached out and put a hand on my back, pulling me to him.

I froze and watched him move closer and closer, knowing what he was about to do but struck with so many emotions, I couldn't react. His nose bumped against mine, I could smell his skin, and suddenly my eyelids were too heavy to stay open.

The next thing I knew, his lips were pressing against mine so that I felt like melting into a puddle on the porch. I lifted one of my hands to touch his face and forgot all about the ton of books in my arms. They crashed to the ground, smashing our toes.

"Ow," Marcus mumbled. "You okay?"

"I think my sneaker is filling with blood," I whispered back.

We laughed, and Marcus finally stepped away. I looked at the mess of books at our feet. "That was some kiss."

He grinned and nudged one of the books with his shoe. "Hopefully it was a little better than Ben's."

"Absolutely." I took his hand. "This time there was no public shame and crying."

We laughed again, and Marcus squeezed my fingers. "Well, I hate to say good-bye. . . ."

"You should go." I nodded. "My stepdad would probably freak if he saw that a boy knew where I lived." I stood on tiptoe and kissed him. "Bye."

He pulled back, wearing a goofy smile. "Bye. I'll see you tomorrow. And don't be too upset about the paper thing. Ava'll get what's coming to her someday."

I watched him jog down the street. "Yes, she will," I murmured. "And that day will be tomorrow."

Gathering all the books and stacking them by the door, I sat on the pile and called Jenner.

"Since my caller ID doesn't say 'County Jail,' I'll assume you haven't done anything crazy yet." She groaned. "Which means you're planning to do it tomorrow."

"That's why I'm friends with you," I said. "You're so smart."

Jenner sighed. "I'm going to try once more to talk you out of this. *Please* just let it go before someone gets hurt."

"Nobody's going to get hurt," I promised. "I'm just going to pull off one mega-prank that'll ensure Ava never messes with me again."

"Well, I'm not helping," she said. "I'm sorry, but I have that tournament coming up and I *cannot* afford to get in trouble."

"Relax." I dug my hand into my pocket and fished out the twenty. "I just need you to come get some money and buy a few things at the grocery store."

Despite her earlier refusal, I could still hear the curiosity in her voice. "The grocery store?"

"Make a list," I said. "Starting with chocolate syrup and Cool Whip. It has to be Cool Whip."

In Jenner's opinion, Brighton Junior Academy before sunrise was the perfect backdrop for a teen horror film. Strange noises echoed in the silence, making vacuum cleaners sound like growling beasts and soft conversation sound like the whisper of wandering spirits.

She cowered behind me as we crept down the hallway, the emergency lights our only guide in the dark.

"I just wanted to let you know," she said, "that if something jumps out at us, I'm going to push you toward it and run. But I will totally come back later and ID your body for the coroner."

"Thanks," I said wryly. "It's so good to have a friend like you."

"Hey, I've already proven what a good friend I am by buying *this* junk." She held up a plastic bag with Cool Whip, chocolate syrup, and a handful of other items. "And after telling you last night that I wasn't going to help, somehow I'm here."

"Only as a lookout," I reminded her. "Now quiet, before someone hears us."

Jenner clamped her mouth shut and crouched even lower, as if that made her invisible. Even though I knew no other student would be crazy enough to get to school so early, I still poked my head into each locker bay before walking past.

When we reached Ava's locker, I cracked the combination, opened the door, and took out all her personal items except one binder . . . her journalism one. I angled it so the higher end faced the inside of her locker and the lower end butted up against the bottom front. Then I reached into a duffel bag I'd brought with me and pulled out a dozen small balloons, all inflated and tied together with a length of transparent thread.

"Hand me the Cool Whip and a spatula, please." I hold out my hand and Jenner passed me the items.

"Is there a reason you said *so* many times that it had to be Cool Whip *and* frozen?" she asked.

I nodded and began spreading the tub of topping over one of the balloons. "It won't melt as quickly as regular whipped cream." I finished with the first balloon and moved on to the second.

"Aha." Jenner laid the bag at my feet. "I think this is the point where I switch to being a lookout."

"Okay, but you're missing all the fu-un," I sang, coating another balloon.

Five minutes later, I held a dozen fluffy white clouds on a string. I added a drizzling of chocolate syrup to the top of them until the whole thing looked almost good enough to eat. Then I worked the thread through one of the top slats of the locker so the balloons were inside and the thread was tied to the outside handle. I stepped back and studied my work. The thread was almost invisible, and if someone were momentarily distracted, they wouldn't even notice.

Next I took a narrow piece of cardboard, bent it in half, and wedged one end in the top of the locker door below Ava's, working the other end so that it stuck out of the bottom slat of Ava's. After giving it a quick test for sturdiness, I reached into my duffel bag and very carefully lifted out a wobbly balloon the size of a cantaloupe.

"*What* is in there?" Jenner hissed from the edge of the locker bay.

I grinned at her. "For instant fun, just add water."

I laid the aquatic bundle behind the cardboard barrier, which held it in place. Then I brought out a second water balloon, propping it behind the first.

With the water balloons secure and the regular balloons tied up in the top of her locker, I closed the door quietly and pulled the cardboard barrier out through the slat.

"That's it?" asked Jenner, coming over to join me. "That's all you're doing?"

"Yep." She didn't need to know about the toothpaste and glitter.

Jenner grinned. "Well, that wasn't nearly as bad as I thought. I may just break out my camera at prank time."

"I'd love it if you would." I gave her a grin of my own, though she couldn't know the added glee behind mine. "Now let's get out of here before someone sees us."

With an hour to go before school started, we ducked into an empty classroom, and Jenner told me the latest good news about her surfing.

"They're going to interview me for a segment on girls who break the gender mold!" she said excitedly. "You know, like you did in your article."

"Only theirs won't be riddled with spelling errors and

incomplete sentences," I said with a smirk.

"Nope," said Jenner. "Because it's a *television* interview!"

I gaped at her. "Jenner! That's so awesome!"

Despite the massive smile on her face, she waved me away. "It's just local, and I'm sure it's partly because of who my dad is, but . . ." She hugged herself. "Yay!"

She filled me in on the details, then nudged my arm. "What about you? When are you going to talk to Katie?"

"I have to take care of that . . ." I checked my watch. Thirty minutes before the first bell. "*Now.*" I got up and gathered my things. "Keep an eye out for Ava and text me the minute she comes into school."

I went in search of Katie and found her surrounded by a circle of Hot Stuff. When they saw me, they attempted to perform a protective Katie barrier, but I broke through it with six simple words.

"We need to talk about Sheldon."

The other members of Hot Stuff looked at one another and Katie with quizzical expressions.

"Who's Sheldon?" one of the girls asked.

Katie ignored her and stepped toward me. "Let's go for a walk."

With the eyes of Hot Stuff burning holes through us, we headed for the picnic tables outside the cafeteria. I sat down, but Katie towered above me, hands on her hips.

"I don't care what you know about Sheldon. Never, ever mention it to me again!" She paused, dropping her arms to her sides. "What *do* you know about Sheldon?"

Over the past week I'd been sifting through the clues I knew about Katie. Then the night before, I'd laid out everything I'd learned and come up with a theory that seemed to explain it all. I just needed a little agreement from Katie.

"I know there was a fire," I said. "I know you were caught in it, and I know someone meant for it to happen." I looked her in the eye. "But I don't think it was you."

Chapter Eighteen

Katie stared at me but didn't speak, so I continued.

"You hung out with bad girls,_ the Harper twins, because you wanted to be one. So, you tried to act the part— dressing trashy, causing trouble . . . and playing with fire. You were *really* good at letting matches burn down, and you loved to show off."

Katie lowered her head and stared at her hands.

"The police found an accelerant at the scene of the fire." I leaned toward her. "Did you know that all it takes is a single spark in that case?

Like . . . from a match someone tosses aside after showing how low they can let it burn?"

She glanced up then, her eyes brimming with tears. "I didn't know! I smelled something, but the twins . . . they—"

"They made up an excuse," I said. "Because they couldn't let you know that before you came in, they'd spread paint thinner or something all over the place. They wanted to burn it down."

Katie dropped onto the bench beside me, crying now. "They set me up! And then they ran! And the . . . the poor turtle was still trapped inside." She hugged her legs to her chest.

"But you rescued it," I said. "And hurt yourself in the process. Not only were your fingerprints on the matches and the turtle tank, but you had burns that proved you were there."

"It was the two of them against me, and I'd already gotten caught with matches after the ban," she sobbed. "Nobody would ever believe I didn't do it."

"Except your parents," I continued. "They convinced the police to drop the case, and you changed schools. In return, you had to get involved in community service to make people aware of the dangers of fire." Katie stopped crying and stared at me. "That's what the NFP is. National Fire Prevention."

"Wow." Katie wiped at her eyes and laughed pitifully. "You really know it all, don't you? And now you're going to tell Paige, so the whole school will find out what a freak I am."

I shook my head. "I'm not going to tell her or anybody else. You are."

Katie's eyes widened and she stared at me, aghast. "No. I can't!"

"Paige thinks you're a threat," I told her. "She's going to come after you until she's humiliated you, but I can keep that from happening if you let me do an interview."

"I'm not ready." She shook her head. "I won't talk."

At that moment, my cell phone buzzed against my hip.

It was showtime.

I took a deep breath and smiled at Katie. "I know this is still haunting you, and it's going to haunt you forever unless you do something about it. Wouldn't you like to stop covering your tracks? Or at least wear T-shirts again?"

Katie bowed her head and stared at the grass. I tried my hardest not to shift from one foot to the other, waiting for her to answer. Finally, she straightened and nodded. "Fine. I'll do the interview."

"You won't regret it." I squeezed her arm and jumped up. "I'll be in touch!"

With a giddy smile I sprinted back into the building,

slowing to a walk as I approached the seventh-grade locker bay. Jenner fell into step beside me, and the two of us did our best to hide our glee when we saw Ava and Ben coming toward us. My heart started beating faster as I reached into my bag and pulled out a white gym towel wrapped in plastic. Just before I'd left for school, I'd squeezed white toothpaste all over one side and dumped an economy-size bottle of iridescent glitter on top. If I kept it out of the light, nobody would suspect a thing.

"Camera ready?" I asked Jenner.

"Set to record every hilarious moment," she replied.

We were close enough now for Ben and Ava to see us. Ben smiled and waved, but Ava stared right through us.

"Hey, Ben!" I said. "Hey, Ava. Planning to steal any more stories today?"

Ben had the nerve to look shocked. "Delilah!"

Ava rested a manicured hand on his arm. "It is fine. Delilah is just confused." She turned to her locker and spun the dial. Her outfit of the day, perhaps inspired by her thievery, was all black, just begging for a dash of something different.

I was more than happy to deliver.

"No," I said. "I'm pretty sure I know what happened. You weren't capable of writing something good, so you stole my work." I nodded to Jenner, who readied her camera. "Is that how you won your Junior Global Journalist Award?"

"You are just a jealous child!" Ava glowered at me, then jerked open her locker door.

A dozen Cool Whip–coated balloons smacked her in the face at the same time the first water balloon rolled down the binder ramp and landed at her feet. It exploded like a small geyser, soaking the bottom half of her pants as she shrieked and fought against the dangling balloons. A second later, water balloon number two rolled down the binder ramp, causing a similar explosion that earned a second shriek from Ava.

Jenner and I burst out laughing as Ava finally slammed her locker door and turned toward us, her face obscured by layers of whipped topping and chocolate syrup.

I grabbed the camera from Jenner and panned over to Ava, waiting for her to launch herself at me for the perfect closing shot. Instead, she just stood there, dripping onto the floor.

Ava stared down at her pants legs for a moment, giving each foot a feeble shake. Then she brought her hands to her face . . . but instead of using them to wipe away the Cool Whip, she pressed them there and sank to the floor.

And she began to cry.

Jenner and I stopped laughing. The camera went into my pocket.

Ava's shoulders quivered as she hiccupped and sobbed, the Cool Whip oozing out between her fingers and falling on her lap.

Ben glared at both of us. "Evil. Both of you. Evil, cruel—" He knelt on the floor beside Ava and hugged her to him.

"Ava, we're so sorry!" Jenner dropped down beside her too. "That was really wrong." She scooped the Cool Whip out of Ava's lap and gave me a distressed look.

I cleared my throat and twisted my hands in front of me. "Ava . . ." The rest of the words got lost somewhere between my brain and my mouth.

Other students were gathering around us now, drawn by Ava's earlier screams. My stomach turned, knowing that where students crowded, teachers followed.

As well as the headmaster.

He pushed his way through the crowd, commanding students to step aside, and when he reached the four of us, his initial reaction was one of stupefied shock.

"What on *earth* happened here?"

Ben, Jenner, and I started talking all at once, hands gesturing wildly, all fingers pointing at me, including my own.

"Delilah, *you* did this?" He shook his head. "But you're normally so levelheaded."

"She stole my article . . . and the newspaper makes me do crazy things," I said meekly.

His face grew hard. "That's not an excuse. However, if it seems to be causing this much trouble, I think you're finished with it."

My mouth fell open, and my forehead wrinkled. "You . . . you can't mean . . ."

"You're off the paper," he said. "And I'll be calling your parents."

"No!" I rushed up to him, gripping his arm. "The paper is my life! You can't take that from me. I'll . . . I'll do anything." I glanced around. "I'll clean the entire school, top to bottom. Or raise money so we can get the new sign board we've been hoping for. Or . . ."

"Delilah"—he pried himself free of me—"no paper." He turned to Jenner. "And you, Miss Jenner . . ."

Her eyes widened in panic, and I stepped in front of her. "She didn't do anything. She was just an innocent bystander."

The headmaster turned to Ben. "Is this true?"

Ben shook his head so hard, I thought he might get whiplash. "She filmed the whole thing."

Without a word I handed the camera to Jenner and she sheepishly handed it to the headmaster.

"We'll be calling your parents too," he told her. Then he offered a free hand to Ava. "Come on, dear. Why don't you get cleaned up so you, Delilah, and I can have a chat in my office."

Ava shook her head and spoke for the first time since the prank. "I don't want anyone else to see me like this. I need—" She looked around, and before I even realized what she was doing, she'd snatched the gym towel from me.

"Wait!" I cried. "Ava, don't—"

It was too late.

Ava rubbed the gooey, glittery side all over her face. Thick smears of white coated her nose, cheeks, and forehead so that they sparkled like Christmas ornaments.

Jenner and Ben gasped. I smacked my forehead with my hand.

"What on *earth*?" said the headmaster again.

Ava took in each of our faces, an expression of terror growing on hers. "What?"

"What *is* this?" Ben took the towel from her and shook it in my face, so blobs of shimmering toothpaste splattered on the ground. "What did you do, Delilah?"

"I . . . um . . . it . . ."

"You told me all you were going to do was the balloons!" Jenner exclaimed. "I can't believe you turned her face into a snow globe!"

"What?!" Ava shrieked and jumped to her feet, running for the bathroom and pushing Jenner out of the way in the process.

"Argh!" Jenner stumbled backward, slipped in the Cool Whip spattering the floor, and landed hard on her arm. It made an audible crunch, and she screamed in pain.

Instantly I was on the ground beside her. "Jenner, are you—"

With her good arm she pushed me hard so that I toppled onto my rear. "Get away from me. I hate you!"

Her words pierced and burned at the same time. "Jenner . . ."

"I told you to stop before someone got hurt. And look who it turned out to be!" She cradled her injured arm and sobbed. "I can't surf in a cast!"

One of the teachers helped her to her feet, and I got up to join them.

"No!" Jenner pushed me again. "Stay away from me!"

She disappeared into the crowd, and then, to make my nightmare complete, Major appeared, his face harsher and angrier than anyone's. "Delilah Elizabeth James!"

My legs, along with my bladder, threatened to give out. "Major! I swear . . ."

"I don't want to hear it!" He stepped in front of me, arms crossed behind his back, upper body stooped so he could force additional air out of his lungs to yell at me. "I just received a phone call from the headmaster at Sheldon. He found one of your notepads in the teacher's lounge. You skipped school to sneak onto their campus and then lied to me about it?" He didn't wait for me to answer. "So, I come here to talk to *your* headmaster and find out you've just assaulted another student—"

"I didn't *assault*—"

"Don't interrupt me when I'm talking!" he snapped. The veins in his forehead throbbed blue. With every word he uttered, I stepped farther and farther away until I'd backed into the corner of the locker bay. "Do you have *any* idea how much trouble you're in?"

This time he stopped talking, and I knew my safest answer would be a nonsarcastic one.

I tried to keep the quaver out of my voice as I said, "A lot, sir."

"Oh, that's an understatement!" He narrowed his eyes at me. "No allowance. No friends. No phone. No life outside of school . . . if they'll even let you keep going here."

"Suspension is definitely a possibility," said the headmaster with a frown.

"Since you've screwed up your life so royally," said Major, "any other crimes I should know about?"

At that moment, Marcus chose to make his appearance.

Since he was taller than most of the students, he was able to see me cowering in the corner, and since he was stronger than most of the students, he was able to push his way to the front.

"Delilah, what's going on?"

Major grabbed Marcus's shoulder before he could reach me. "Who are you?"

Marcus gave him an evil look and jerked free. "I'm her boyfriend. Back off."

Of all the times he could have chosen to declare our relationship status, he chose that moment. The fates clearly had it in for me.

Major looked as if Marcus had slapped him. "I recognize you. You're a red border!"

"A *what*?"

Instead of explaining, Major cast dooming eyes on me. "You're dating someone I expressly forbade you to date?"

Marcus frowned at me. "What's he talking about, Delilah?"

"I . . . I . . ." I looked from him to the headmaster to Ben to Major, their faces all melting into one giant blur of tears.

I'd lost my paper. My best friend hated me. My soon-to-be stepfather would never trust me again. My first boyfriend was about to be my first *ex*-boyfriend. And on top of all *that*, half the school was watching my self-destruction—and no doubt loving it.

My heart throbbed in my ears. I blinked several times and tried to speak, but suddenly it felt like my head was clouded with cotton, and I found it hard to focus. And then all the light went out of the world and I felt the cold squish of Cool Whip beneath me.

Chapter Nineteen

I woke up in a way I hoped would never happen again . . . with my face in the sweaty armpit of the school nurse. She was leaning across me for something and jumped back when I let out a startled scream.

"Major Paulsen," she said, clutching her chest, "I believe Delilah's awake."

Major was standing beside my cot in a matter of seconds, his bushy eyebrows wiggling furiously, as if he wasn't sure whether to be mad or relieved or concerned.

I reached out for his hand. "Please

don't yell. I know I messed up big-time."

His eyebrows relaxed and he squeezed my fingers. "There won't be any more yelling. I think you've had enough for one day."

I closed my eyes, remembering the crowd of students who now knew all the horrible things I'd done. "I got what I deserved."

Major pulled a chair up beside my cot. "And what makes you say that?"

Behind him, I could see Jenner sitting on another cot, her arm in a sling. My lower lip trembled, so I couldn't speak. Instead, I just pointed.

Major glanced over his shoulder at Jenner, and she looked at him, avoiding direct eye contact with me.

"Ah. I see," said Major. "Well, that was an unfortunate consequence, yes."

"I turned Ava into a laughingstock and made her cry." I started crying myself. "And I snuck out of school and lied to you and ruined my best friend's life." I breathed deeply and choked a little. "I'm a monster!"

Major handed me a tissue. "First, there are no such things as monsters, so you most certainly aren't one. Second, why did you do all that?"

I took the tissue from him but merely clutched at it, wiping my eyes on my sleeve. "I wanted to win the war."

"You wanted . . ." Major trailed off and pressed his hands together, bringing them to his lips. "That was why you came to me."

I nodded. "You said Ava was the enemy, and that I had to neutralize the threat."

"Of course." Now Major closed his eyes, shaking his head. "That was some . . . terrible parenting on my part."

"No!" I sat up on my cot. "It's my fault—"

Major stopped me with a raised hand. "Delilah, I talked to you as if you were one of my men. I didn't stop to think how different the world works for someone your age. I should never have compared your situation to mine."

His eyes narrowed and he frowned. "Of course, I may have handled things differently if I'd known *exactly* what was going on. Telling someone you're doing a project on war is much different from telling them you're going to wage war, isn't it?"

I sniffled and nodded again. "Yes, sir."

Major got to his feet and paced beside my cot. "In the future you will stick to the *whole* truth about a problem, and you will tell an adult how you plan to solve it."

"Yes, sir."

"You will also . . ." He paused, glancing down at the way his hands were folded behind his back. "I'm doing it again."

For the first time since I'd woken up, I smiled. "A little."

Major let his shoulders drop enough to look sad but not sloppy. "You know, I've always excelled in every field. I was top of my class at West Point, and I mastered night drops in jump school before anyone else. But being a father . . ." He held his arms out, as if expecting to be handed the Worst Parent of the Year Award. Instead, I leaned into the empty space and hugged him.

"You're going to be a great dad," I said. "Because you always want what's best for me."

"I do," he agreed, squeezing me. "Even if my efforts are . . . slightly misguided."

I leaned back. "And I still would have tried to beat Ava with or without your advice. Because I want the best for me too."

"But you shouldn't have to hurt other people to get it." Across the room, Jenner finally spoke, though it was directed at the floor.

I slid off the cot and approached her cautiously, but she didn't move to stop me. "I know." I sat beside her. "You were right . . . about everything. I should have just let Ava have the position."

Now Jenner glanced up, shaking her head vigorously. "No, Delilah. I never said that. You should *totally* be the lead reporter, and I still think you deserve it more than Ava does."

"Thanks." I ventured a small smile. "But I'm sure you would have preferred I not break your arm in the process."

"Well, duh. But lucky for you"—Jenner raised her slung arm—"it's not broken. Just bruised."

I fell back against the cot in relief. "I thought I heard it crunch!"

With a sheepish grin she reached into her pants pocket and pulled out a cracked container of mints. "The bad news . . . my Tic Tacs are now in powder form. The good news . . . I can still surf."

I gave a happy squeal and hugged her. She returned it, and when we pulled apart, I crossed my heart with my fingers. "I promise I'll never do anything to put you or our friendship in danger again."

Jenner repeated my gesture. "I promise to never let you." We smiled at each other, and I turned to Major.

"And I promise to tell you *everything* when I'm in trouble . . . but only if we can get rid of the banned boy book." I felt myself blushing. "There are guys in there you've . . . you've color-coded unfairly."

Major raised an eyebrow. "I suppose you're referring to the red border around that young man who calls himself your boyfriend."

My cheeks warmed even more, but I nodded. "He's really nice. And he's changed a lot over the last year."

"So I've read." Major nodded to a copy of the *Brighton Bugle* sitting on the counter. "I'm not sure how much of it to believe, but you wrote a compelling article, at least."

"Oh, it's all true," I said. "I fact-checked everything." It took a moment for his last words to sink in. "Wait." I frowned. "How did you know I wrote it? I never mentioned it, and Ava's name is on the byline."

"I've seen enough of your work to recognize your style." He cleared his throat. "Also, Jenner told me."

I looked at her and she nodded. "I told the headmaster, too, when he came to check on you. And Paige stopped by and told him Ava's been bragging about the whole thing, so he's *really* upset with her."

I sat in stunned silence, cycling through everything I'd just heard. "Paige stuck up for me? Jenner, *you* stuck up for me? Even when you were mad?"

Jenner smiled and bumped me with her shoulder. "Well, of course. You're my best friend."

I hugged her again. "This is a horrible question to ask right now, but"—I glanced hopefully at Major—"do you think the headmaster might let me back on the paper? Since it wasn't entirely my fault?"

Major smiled, as if he'd been waiting for that question. "The three of us will sit down and talk. I'm sure we can come up with something, even if it's probationary."

I gave him my most wide-eyed, innocent look. "Does that mean I can get out of being grounded, too?"

"Ha!" Major slapped me on the shoulder. "Never in a thousand years."

When I was allowed to leave the nurse's office a half hour later, the first thing I did was send a text to Marcus, asking him to meet me in the courtyard. Since it was between classes, I snuck outside without too many people watching, which was a good thing. I'd been the center of attention enough for one day.

As soon as I saw Marcus, I dropped onto one of the benches and clasped my hands in my lap. "Hey."

He sat beside me. "Hey. Are you okay? I went by the office to check on you earlier, but you were still out of it."

"I'm fine," I said, glowing a little at his concern. "I just needed to tell you something, and you might not like me after you hear it."

Marcus bowed his head and leaned forward. "Is this the breakup talk?"

"No!" I grabbed one of his hands and held it tight. "I mean, you might want to when I'm finished, but . . . but *I* don't want to."

"Okay." Marcus gave me a curious smile. "Who did you murder?"

I told him everything I'd done, from the Renee Mercer incident on. A couple times he smiled, but most of the time he sat quietly and shook his head. When I felt like I'd reached the end of my story, I let go of his hand and took a deep breath.

"Well . . . now you know what kind of person I am."

Instead of storming off in disgust, Marcus busted out laughing. "Delilah, I've *always* known what kind of person you are."

I squinted at him, not sure if I should be offended or relieved. "You have?"

"Yes!" He took my hand. "You want to win at everything, but sometimes you don't think about how you're getting there. It doesn't mean you're a bad person."

I blushed and nodded. "Thanks . . . for not hating me."

"Everybody makes mistakes," he said with a grin. "Yours are just more exciting."

He leaned over and kissed me, and I hugged him tight.

"I'm dropping the whole issue with Katie," I mumbled into his shoulder.

Marcus leaned back. "*Not* because of me."

I rolled my eyes. "Of course not. And not because of anybody else, either. I just . . . I know people will treat her differently if they find out."

Marcus smiled. "Cool."

I wanted to stay with him all afternoon, but I was sure that Major would come looking for me and wouldn't be thrilled to find Marcus attached to my face. So, I gave him one last kiss and said good-bye. I would, after all, see him the next morning . . . along with the rest of the school.

Major let me stay home for the afternoon, but I knew I had to go back the next morning or risk becoming a seventh-grade dropout. Jenner waited for me by the front doors, and the two of us braved the hall and the dozens of staring eyes that watched to see what excitement we'd cause next.

"I feel like one of those celebrities caught in some major scandal," I whispered to Jenner.

"*I* feel like we're the last humans in a school full of zombies, and they're just waiting to catch us off guard and eat our brains." I gave her a look and she shrugged. "*Dawn of the Dead* was on last night."

"Okay, then." I scooted closer to her, doing my best not to meet any of the intense stares. "How much longer do you think we'll feel like celebrities slash zombie bait?"

"Only until the next major scandal hits our school. Maybe we should convince that juvie girl to go public. Ooh!" She grabbed my arm. "Or maybe you can get Katie to come clean about her pyro past."

I shook my head. "It really is her story to tell when she's ready. I'm not going to push her."

"Aww." Jenner squeezed me. "Look at you! Caring about other people. Between you and Paige, it almost feels like Christmas."

"Speaking of Paige." I nodded down the hall where she was leaning against her locker, filing her nails. "I should probably go thank her."

Jenner and I walked up to Paige, but before I could say anything, Paige spoke first.

"I hear Ava's sparkling personality is really showing." She glanced up from her perfectly rounded nails and smirked. "Not that I've had a chance to judge for myself. Apparently, she's not coming back until next week."

I nodded. "Until then, I'll be thinking of ways to apologize that won't end with her spitting in my face."

"Good." Paige returned her nail file to her locker. "Then you'll be too busy to think about the bad news I have to give you."

"Let me guess." I squinted and massaged the sides of my skull. "I'm no longer eligible for the Debutantes."

She sighed and patted my shoulder. "Sorry. But if you want, you can still tell me what you learned about Katie." She gave me her most winning smile, complete with toothpaste-commercial gleam.

I sighed and patted her shoulder. "Sorry. Not gonna happen, but I *can* tell you she didn't get invited to any Nouveau Fashion premiere."

Paige thought about it for a second and shrugged. "Good enough for me."

"Are you guys going to give the spot to Ava, then?" Jenner asked her.

"Actually," said Paige, "the Debutantes talked, and we decided not to include a member of the newspaper staff. We realized that Ava and Delilah would do more harm for our reputation than good."

"That's true," I said. "Especially since I plan to behead a live chicken in the cafeteria for an encore."

"Oh. Heh-heh." Paige laughed nervously and looked around. "Listen, Delilah," she said in a low voice, "I like you as a person. And Jenner, I bothered to learn how to say your name, so that should tell you something."

"Definitely," said Jenner, winking at me.

"Great." Paige clapped her hands together. "Then you'll both understand that even though we might be friends . . . I can't be seen with you right now. Not until the whole thing with Delilah blows over, anyway." Paige winced and bit her lip. "You understand, right?"

"Of course." I elbowed Jenner and she nodded solemnly. "It was very noble of you to risk your reputation just to tell us *this* much."

Paige rolled her eyes and grunted. "You guys think I'm shallow, don't you?"

"Only as shallow as a wading pool," I assured her. Paige opened her mouth for an argument, but I stopped her. "I'm kidding. You were nice enough to defend me in front of the headmaster. We shouldn't expect you to do too much at once."

"Yeah, we're just hoping that by next semester, you'll still remember we're in the same grade," agreed Jenner.

Paige looked pained but backed away. "Okay. I guess . . . bye for now. And good luck with your lives."

As Paige hurried away, Jenner turned to me and smiled. "'Bye for now and good luck with your lives.' She should write greeting cards."

"I should have known it wouldn't last," I said. "My hair clashed with everything in her wardrobe."

Jenner sighed and rubbed her bruised arm. "Well, you didn't get into the Little Debbies. . . ."

"Nope."

"You didn't steal Ben away from Ava. . . ."

I shook my head. "If anything, I brought them closer together."

"And if you're lucky, you'll be a probationary member of the newspaper."

I rubbed my hands together. "All in all, I'd say a pretty successful start to the school year."

Jenner laughed. "Was it seriously worth it?"

"Well . . ." I thought about everything that had happened recently—the people I'd gotten to know, the *good* things I'd done and learned . . . none of which would have happened if it hadn't been for Ava and the newspaper. "It was totally worth it," I said. "Although, if I could have changed one thing . . ."

"Yeah?"

I wrinkled my nose. "I would *never* have worn your gym clothes."

Do you love the color pink?
All things sparkly? Mani/pedis?

These books are for you!